Jane Thomas

Autumnal leaves

elegiac and other poems

Jane Thomas

Autumnal leaves
elegiac and other poems

ISBN/EAN: 9783337374457

Printed in Europe, USA, Canada, Australia, Japan

Cover: Foto ©Andreas Hilbeck / pixelio.de

More available books at **www.hansebooks.com**

AUTUMNAL LEAVES.

Elegiac and other Poems.

BY

MRS. ~~EDWARD~~ Jane THOMAS,

AUTHOR OF "TRANQUIL HOURS," "SIR REDMOND," "THE MERCHANT'S DAUGHTER
OF TOULON," ETC., ETC., ETC.

" To our places in the vineyard of our God return we now,
    With kindled eye, with onward step, with hand upon the plough;
    Our hearts are safer anchored, our hopes have richer store:
    One treasure more in Heaven is ours, one bright example more."

THE REV. HENRY ALFORD, DEAN OF CANTERBURY.

LONDON:
W. WALKER AND CO., 196, STRAND.

MDCCCLX.

TO

The Memory

OF

A BELOVED AND ONLY CHILD,

These Poems

ARE INSCRIBED BY HIS WIDOWED AND SORROWING MOTHER,

IN THE EARNEST AND HUMBLE HOPE

THAT THEY DO NOT CONTAIN ONE SENTIMENT THAT CAN BE

REPUGNANT TO THE INNATE PURITY,

WHICH IS NOW MADE PERFECT IN HEAVEN.

PREFACE.

———

" On the 29th ult., at Rolleston Hall, in this county,
to the inexpressible grief of his widowed mother, and
the deep regret of all who knew him, EDWARD HARRY
THOMAS, the only child of the late Rev. EDWARD
THOMAS, and Captain in the Leicestershire Militia,
in the thirtieth year of his age."—LEICESTERSHIRE
GUARDIAN, *February 5th*, 1859.

" DEATH OF CAPTAIN THOMAS.—Our Obituary of
to-day, records a death which will cause deep regret
both in this town and county — that of Captain
THOMAS, of the Leicestershire Militia. Beloved

wherever he was known, this amiable young man is cut off in the very flower of his age, with prospects as bright as his best friends could wish for him; for he was heir presumptive to extensive landed estates, and on the point of forming a matrimonial alliance with one of our oldest county families.

"To his brother officers, and to all who had the pleasure of his acquaintance, Captain THOMAS's loss will be grievous—what must it be to her who has so long watched over him with such maternal devotedness, and to her who was so soon to be his bride? When we say he was 'the only child of his mother and she is a widow, beside him she had neither son nor daughter,' we feel we need not add another word to show the extent of the bereavement. His remains were consigned to the ancestral vault in the little church at Billesdon, amid the tears of his affectionate relatives, the attached tenantry of the estate, and the domestics of the Hall."—*Ibid.*

Not another word, indeed, need be added to show the extent of the bereavement! The foregoing affecting record must speak to the hearts of every one who is touched with even a feeling of common humanity. I will only then remark that, with the exception of the first six, these Poems were all written long before I even imagined such a total wreck of earthly happiness; yet, from their tone of pervading sadness, it would seem that I unconsciously did "rejoice with trembling" over the treasure—

"Not dead, but gone before."

J. THOMAS.

CONTENTS.

I. In Memoriam.

II. Occasional Poems.

The first six Poems, marked by asterisks, have been written since the death of my most-loved and ever-to-be-regretted son. How faintly do they portray the deep anguish of my heart! But

" Slow comes the verse that *real* woe inspires."

AUTUMNAL LEAVES.

I. In Memoriam.

MY SON.

"Now when he came nigh to the gate of the city, behold, there was a dead man carried out, the only son of his mother, and she was a widow,"—St. Luke vii. 12.

In his own image, God created him,
  And spotless kept him in his birth-hour state ;
Letting no stain the excellence bedim,
  Which He preserved, for Heaven, immaculate.

To show how perfect here a man could be,
  Upon the earth he long enough remained ;
While I made conscious, gracious God, by Thee,
  Not unawares an angel entertained ;

B

For, oh! so reverential was my love,
    So holy, so devout each sentiment;
I felt, of right, his dwelling was above:
    And he to me was but in pity lent.

My son! my son! my ever-new delight!
    My rapture, ever with fresh ardour sought!
How thou hast vanished from my watchful sight,
    Hast filled with wonder my astonished thought!

I strive to pray—I strive to reconcile
    My shattered happiness with God's decree;
Then flashes on my soul thy glowing smile:
    And all my anguish is renewed for thee!

Pardon the widow, Lord! whose only son
    Thou didst not rescue from the sepulchre:
Have patience, Lord! in time " Thy will be done,"
    May burst in resignation, even from her.

My faith, like Abraham's, Thou didst not test,

   To guerdon it with most divine surprise ;

Thou knewest, Lord! the weakness unconfest :

   So took, unasked, my lamb of sacrifice.

My son! who standest now at God's right hand,

   My angel-son! in glory's robes arrayed ;

My son! the foremost now in Mercy's band :

   Remember me, when I shall need thy aid.

May it be soon! I weary of my woe,

   Life is too burthensome to bear alone ;

Oh! I felt nothing, when thou wert below,

   Save love's warm atmosphere which round me shone.

Now all oppresses ; for, the heavy air

   Comes loaded with the vapours of the grave ;

Oh! would that I were hidden from my care

   In that still darkness, wounded spirits crave.

Had I been proud—as many would have been,
    Possessing thee—I had deserved this blow;
But I sought earnestly each troubled scene,
    Where tears of agony did fastest flow; .

To weep with them that wept—to pour the oil,
    That heals the smartings hurry on decay;
Oh! never once did my glad soul recoil
    From the pale anguish which affrights the gay;

To show the silver lining in each cloud,
    To eyes, would scarcely in its light believe;
Yet, for all this, my son! thou'rt in thy shroud :
    So God refused the offering to receive.

My son! enlist the seraphs on my side,
    With thee let all the heavenly hosts implore;
That thy poor mother's struggles with the tide
    Of whelming sorrow may be shortly o'er :—

Thou canst not cross the everlasting bourne,

   Howe'er thy soul may yearn to comfort me ;

Yet—yet a gleam of hope, the while I mourn,

   Rises amid despair's obscurity,

Suffusing with celestial ray the gloom

   Which I must brave, my son! how fearlessly!—

To seek beyond the barrier of the tomb,

   The consummation of God's clemency!

Would, that my hour were come! would I could meet

   My son, my Saviour, and my Judge benign ;

My son! my son! embracing Jesu's feet, .

   Having no sins to own, entreat for mine ;

That when I, panting, reach the crystal gates,

   Whose entrance opens on eternity ;

Only the welcome, which the blest awaits,

   May greet thy mother, from her God, and—thee !

ONCE MORE, MY SON! ONCE MORE!

"The heart knoweth his own bitterness; and a stranger doth
not intermeddle with his joy."—PROVERBS xiv. 10.

THE Lord, He gave—and lo! the Lord His treasure

    does retake;

Yet, though bowed to the very earth, my faith this

    shall not shake;

What! shall I good from God receive, and shall I evil

    shun?

How could I hope life's rock-bound sea would ever

    smoothly run?

What years of happiness were mine! How trembles

    now my soul,

As memory brings the transports back, then under no

    control!

No fears to cast a damp on them ; no doubts, lest they
 should fade ;

Ere I, though clinging to them still, within the tomb
 was laid.

Till restitution was required, then, midst deep
 mysteries,

What sobs convulsed my stifled breast ; what tears
 obscured mine eyes ;

And agony so shook my frame, I tottered in each limb ;

As yet I hurried frantic on, to look my last on him ;

The idol of so many years, the worshipped of each
 hour ;

The bud—the blossom of my soul—my one love-
 cultured flower—

The only child me mother called—and oh ! in such a
 tone,

God never heard a sweeter one, from seraphs round
 His throne.

Ah! only they who've gazed their last on him they'd
  died to save;

Ah! only they whose desperate grief would hold him
  from the grave;

Ah! only they whose maddened brain denies he dead
  can be,

Can comprehend—and faintly too—my incredulity.

The vision vanished which, to me, was real as the
  light

That ushers in the new-born day, from the dark womb
  of night;

Yea, Lord! as real as the creed, that firmly I believe,

Which teaches Thou dost love them most, whom most
  Thou dost aggrieve :—

And his young love—his destined bride—she! she
  who'd scarcely erred,

Why were the waters of her soul by the death-angel
  stirred?

Why did they overwhelm the hope, whose crescent
    softly rose
In sky as calmly beautiful, as met the eyes of those
Who first in admiration gazed on the azure vault
    serene,
Before they knew through it, (how soon,) would
    tempests intervene ?—

When all was o'er—most sacredly on his dead heart
    I placed
The letters where her artless love she guilelessly had
    traced ;
Resolved no mortal eye save his their tenderness
    should know ;
Though purest angel would not blush, could he those
    letters show
In that chaste Heaven, where all is pure, where all is
    undefiled ;
Where artifice has never yet one sinless saint beguiled;

Where love is simple as a babe, all smiles of joyousness,

And God, who is Himself but Love, does heap it to
excess!

All festivals—all holy days—all days of jubilee—

Will now be held as funeral ones—my precious son!
by me;

Once shared by thee—oh! how could I alone keep,
otherwise

Than as re-burials of the dead, such hallowed revelries?

I would be still, but this loud world, with ever-start-
ling sound,

Mocking the cry of "Peace, peace, peace," where
peace cannot be found,

Distracts my bosom—breaks the hush, which steals,
like drowsiness,

Upon the worn and weary heart, exhausted by
distress.

How I have sorrowed for my son—God! well Thou
　knowest how!
Yet would I, selfish, snatch the crown of glory from
　his brow?
No:—let him wear it like a king—a heaven-anointed
　king:
Yet, Lord! permit o'er me he spreads a fond pro-
　tecting wing,
To shield me from the bitter blasts that chill my
　wasted frame,
Until the mandate comes to me which, Lord! unto
　him came;
How welcome in my loneliness! how will I bare my
　breast
To meet the arrow, (mercy-sped,) which brings the
　restless rest!

MY SON'S BETROTHED.

" Our first love murder'd is the sharpest pang
The human heart can feel. . . . ."
YOUNG'S " Brothers."

ERE, bud of hope, through time, one leaf has shed,

   She's learnt the uttermost of human grief;

Alas ! the pity ! that, for her, instead

   Of youth's expectancy, the tried belief,

Love, the hoped substance of life's sole delight,

Proves but the shadow of its woful night.

    The " passing-bell "—yea—be it tolled,

      'Tis muffled for her ear ;

    Who now, in passion uncontrolled,

      Sheds desperation's tear;

No merry peal of marriage gay,
  But that oppressive sound
Which tells a soul has passed away,
  To mystery profound.—
Who durst admonish such a grief?—
  Who reckon it a crime?—
O, what a wretched make-belief
  Reproof, at such a time!

Then—let her agony have vent;
  Such agony must rave;
'Tis useless urging—" It is sent
  To purify, and save;"
To one who could not, would not hear,
  Even though an angel spoke;
No—not if he, from highest sphere,
  Her patience did invoke;
Whose loss occasioned her despair,
  Her mental overthrow:

A time will come for calmer prayer;

For calmer tears to flow.—

Ah ! what a change !—ah ! what a change,

For one so young to feel !

Nought can, on earth, her soul estrange

From him, who makes appeal

Each hour to it—in every scene—

In dreams—when she can sleep :—

And, if awake—the " what has been"

Thoughts of the time will keep,

When time was counted by the heart,

Which chid each brief delay;

As if, from life, some vital part

Of joy were held at bay;—

When expectation from the eye

Glanced, like a rippling stream,

Illuminated from a sky

Of cloudless solar beam ;—

When hope upon the severed lips,

   In breathless rapture, hung ;

While shyness every sentence clips

   That fluttered from the tongue ;—

When ecstacy's impassioned thrill

   Each pulse did animate :—

And—now the soul that stands so still :—

   Arrested thus by Fate !

O God ! why suffer them to meet,

   To part through such a blow ?

O God ! O God ! how incomplete

   Is happiness below !—

To that reiterated " Why?"

   Thou ne'er hast yet replied ;

Love still must see fond lovers die,

   As lovers fond have died ;

And love, through life, must drag about

   A chain, whose links but gall ;

Yet—with a tenderness devout,

　Them the heart's jewels call.—

Ah! with her love within the tomb,

　With memories ne'er to cease;

She's listening for the voice of doom,

　As agony's release;—

But Death accedes not when implored,

　Woe must his will abide;

Else the adoring, and adored,

　Had slumbered side by side.—

Her grief, which now so real seems,

　Her poignancy of thought;

Shall they be held but idle dreams,

　That torture life for nought?

The tears so passionate and strong,

　The sighs, the bosom rend;

Esteem we them, at last, too wrong

　For reason to defend?

Lo, God, who wipes all tears away,

Even God, who prompts each prayer,

Forbears to exercise His sway,

Till time shall grief prepare

To feel—to own the stroke was just,

Yea—merciful, in sooth;

Which levelled Hope, even with the dust,

To raise it up as Truth.

Shall man then prematurely preach,

While God remaineth mute?

The lessons, which his silence teach,

Man's eloquence confute.

For He who made the suffering heart,

Its sorrows well may scan,

And bear the expression of their smart,

More patiently than man.

Poor, stricken one!—a few more tears,

A few more hopes unblest;

A few more disappointing years,

 And thou wilt be at rest.

Thy Saviour has downtrod the thorns,

 Which choked thy path to God;

And thou, whose sorrow Jesus mourns,

 Must tread the way He trod;

To bear thy cross up Calvary,

 Whose glorious heights, when gained,

Thy soul may shout exultingly,

 "Salvation is attained!"

Which angels catching, shall repeat,

 While one (how instant known!)

To heaven his looked-for bride shall greet,

 In earth's familiar tone!

MY SON'S FIRST BIRTHDAY AFTER DEATH.

"A good name is better than precious ointment; and the day of death than the day of one's birth."—ECCLESIASTES vii. 1.

"He answered me and said, This present life is not the end where much glory doth abide."—2 ESDRAS vii. 42.

OH ! if in the abodes of perfect bliss,

To which thou wert translated suddenly,

Remembrance is allowed of world like this;

On me bestow that filial memory :—

Or rather, with impartial love, divide

That consciousness, between thy mother here,

And the nipped flower, who hoped to be thy bride :

Ere summoned hence wert thou from hearts so dear.

Her head is bowed, my son ! her heart is broke ;

　　She pines to share thy everlasting rest ;

While my own tears, the words of·comfort choke,

　　For her sole soothing, I would have expressed.—

My son, my son, forlorn enough are we,

　　Blasted like trees, upon storm-smitten heath ;

Yet gratefully, our heavenward glances see

　　Thy brow encircled with Redemption's wreath.—

Oh, supplicate, my son ! the angel-throng,

　　Who celebrate with thee thy natal day ;

To plead for pardon, if the grief is wrong :

　　Which over us bears such tyrannic sway.—

No : name it not—let nought terrestrial jar

　　The heavenly harmony attuned for thee ;

Earth,.and its earthly anguish, must not mar

　　Thy full fruition of felicity.

The requiem of our untamed despair

　　Must mingle not with music of the sky ;

Lest, in the lull of gladder harpings there,

Thine ear should catch its mournful minstrelsy,

And recognise our birthday hymn for thee,

Dirgelike, and solemn, as funereal wail;

And dissonance be blent with melody :

Whose diapason should serene prevail.

Oh ! as the years, love-registered, brought round

The happy birthdays, welcomed so by me ;

My soul, enamoured, bathed in the profound

Of an immeasurable ecstacy ;

Yet—forced was I "with trembling to rejoice,"

To lighten bonds, seemed slackening every hour ;

Yet forced was I to ask, in doubtful voice,

Of Him, o'er fate has absolutest power ;

" How long, O Lord ! how long will this endure ?

O Lord, in loving mercy answer me !—

Lord ! wilt Thou not a mother's hope ensure ?—

The sweetest hope, she could receive from Thee."—

Was the Lord angered?—did I wrath provoke,

   That He so sternly unto me replied?—

Crushing, with one annihilating stroke,

   Me, and, alas! thy unoffending bride?

Her grief, how great!—and oh! how great is mine!—

   We have not courage to compare our woes!—

Yet, with the heartstrings, stronger doth entwine

   The love, from infancy, that ever grows:—

Mine then is greatest; for I grieve for both;

   While she, completely occupied with thee,

(Though liberal as charity,) feels loth,

   To spend regret upon my agony:—

In Nature, what a gap thy death has made,

   And, in our bosoms, what a vacancy;

While we go timidly, as if afraid

   Of some untoward new calamity!

Yet—what misfortune can us now befall ?—

Has sorrow from us one affliction kept ?—

Why, if destruction did the world o'er-pall,

Our dead we've buried—and our dead we've wept.

And now, like pilgrims who have reached the shrine,

By superhuman hope encouraged on ;

Where is to end life's trials, they resign

To Christ the staff of faith, they lean upon ;

We're bowing down in prayer, hand clasped in hand,

And souls resolved, as martyrs, to depart ;

Longing to feel the soaring wings expand,

To mount to realms, where thou already art !

OH! HOW I YEARN FOR THEE, MY SON!

"Weeping may endure for a night, but joy cometh in the morning."—PSALM xxx. 5.

"Let me die the death of the righteous, and let my last end be like his!"—NUMBERS xxiii. 10.

My tearful eyes to heaven I raise,

   In sorrow's vague desire to see

What never more, to human gaze,

   Apparent, O my son! can be.—

And then, with morbid wish, I crave,

   (For thought on something sure to dwell,)

To penetrate into thy grave;

   And ransack its mysterious cell.

Yet—what does now that grave contain
  To captivate a mother's love ?—
O Jesus !—pardon—and sustain
  The soul, that sighs to meet above
The beauty, which was so extreme ;
  The worth, surpassing all compeers ;
The piety, should form the theme
  Of exultation—not these tears.—

Yet—thou—while on the earth—who weptst,
  Subdued to mortal agony ;
And by the grave of friendship, keptst
  The vigil of humanity ;—
Thou—who couldst cry, in mortal woe,
  "Father ! allow this cup to pass !"
When traitor friend—and open foe,
  Exposed Thee to a ribald mass ;—
Canst comprehend that mortal throe,
  Which wrings the soul, despair has fed ;

And suffer mortal tears to flow,

    Which but for mortal pangs are shed ;—

Canst suffer suffering to try,

    To hold communion with thy saints ;

While hope, on retroverted eye,

    The glory of submission paints,

To lead dejection such as mine,

    To look beyond earth's transient ills ;

And learn to own that the Divine

    Is merciful in all He wills ;—

Canst suffer me to breathe the strain

    Of ineffectual distress ;

(Until I learn to joy in pain;

    And own that pain a nothingness,)

Unto the dead.

          Yet to the dead,

    Wherefore even sorrow's vain appeal ?—

The dead—whose consciousness has fled,

    Oh! can it sympathise—or—feel ?—

'Tis to the living, Jesus ! Thou
  Didst triumph over Death, to save,
That grief should speak, as I do now ;
  Not to dead ashes, in the grave :
Therefore, my son ! to thee I send
  My tale of hapless misery ;
Whose sanctioned spirit may attend :
  Sanctioned, my grief to sanctify.

Oh ! till I wept thee, on thy bier,
  Oh ! till I saw thee borne away ;
I knew not how deserted here
  I should become, from day to day.
Still must I tell each thought to thee,
  For—oh ! each thought is wholly thine ;
Thou—when an infant at my knee :
  (And purity did thee enshrine,)
In thy untarnished innocence,
  Hadst not, even then, one thought more free

From earthly vice—from earth's offence,

Than those I utter now to thee.

Thou'rt never absent from my sight;

Thou art in each familiar place,

Like golden track, that's very bright,

My path to heaven direct to trace;

The echo of thy infant joy,

Above all other sounds, I hear;

When thy first laugh had no alloy:

No moral maxim, clothed in fear;

And then thy manhood's firmer tone,

To speak protectingly still seems;

I turn to answer—but alone

I find myself, with idlest dreams;

I pray for thee—how vain, how vain—

For thee!—for whom a Saviour prays!—

Yet—darling! how can I refrain

From such sweet long-accustomed ways?—

I weep for thee—how vainer still—

    For thee !—whose tears a Saviour dries !

Yet—yet my heart, like mountain-rill,

    Fresh sources for my tears supplies.

Oh ! mine is a true woman's grief,

    Which only is expressed by tears ;

With vivid intervals, most brief,

    Of former too enchanting years.

I cannot rave—nor rend my hair—

    Nor act like Tragedy insane—

Mine's not the frenzy of despair,

    Would call thee from the tomb again ;

It is that sensibility,

    On which a God in judgment sits ;

And, though almost idolatry,

    In His staid wisdom, He permits ;

Which, bound to earth, tenacious clings

    To earth's illusory deceit ;

Nor seems aware—remembrance brings

    But visions which the senses cheat ;

And these the visions now pourtrayed,

   By retrospection's life-like sketch ;

My son ! ere hope was death-betrayed :

   Or I became this lonely wretch ;

When thou didst leave—then hurry back,

   Nor novelty could thee seduce ;

While never did my welcome lack

   The ardour, might have cooled from use.

From that abandoned spot named home,

   (From which I did in horror flee ;)

Despatches, as of old, still come :

   But no fond messages from thee ;

The silence of the grave does rest

   Upon thy filial tenderness ;

Yet every word to me addressed,

   Upon my heart, with pointed stress

Is written, by undying love,

   To which I turn—as sacred lore ;

To read of one—a saint above,

    Who wrote to me those words of yore.

'Tis better thus to think—and weep—

    Yea—even in undue excess—

Than leave the stagnant soul to creep

    Into entire forgetfulness—

It should " remember such things were,

    Which were, indeed, to it most dear;"

Nor from their reminiscence spare

    One memory-exacting tear;

For thought, when on an angel bent,

    From worldly dross must sifted be;

And lose that impious discontent,

    Which sours, and sharpens God's decree.

O Christ! how have I tried to think

    As Thou wouldst have my thoughts incline;

And, with unwavering faith, to drink
    Life's draught of sacramental wine;
Oh! teach me how I may attain
    Unto my son's celestial state!—
Oh! teach me, Lord! how I may gain
    The pardon, Lord! for which I wait!—
Hast Thou not taught me? Lord! I know,
    I must no longer sorrow here,
For him, with that usurping woe,
    To Thee may criminal appear;
But hope—yea, hope—through Mercy's grace,
    (How longs my soul, at this, to die!)
Again to see him face to face:
    And Thou, too, Lord! in realms on high!—
O come! Lord Jesus! quickly come;
    My spirit wearies, Lord! for Thee
To guide it where my son, at home,
    Impatient is to welcome me!

VIOLETS FROM MY SON'S BETROTHED.

" Pray to live
So fair and innocently ; pray to die,
Leaf after leaf, so softly."—DEATH'S JEST BOOK.

THE violets, so fresh from thee,

Though perished, treasured are by me,

For the emotions they impart,

To wound, yet meliorate the heart ;

From pleasure, wedded unto pain,

No more to be divorced again.—

Sad bridals !—where the smile and tear

In union, all too close, appear !—

They died—as vividness should die,

Which mocks this life-suspecting eye !—

D

They died—as bloom should speed away,

In earth's swift hurry of decay ;

To prove, with startling emphasis,

Duration's not for world like this,

Where loveliness does soonest fade ;

Which lasting but for Heaven is made !—

Ah ! dearest ! what a fate is ours,

When, to us, Nature's simplest flowers

Come with remembrance on each leaf,

There written by the hand of grief !—

Yet—yet—though hard to learn, the wise

Protest, such lesson we should prize,

As teachings from a God of love ;

Who breathes instruction from above,

Through sorrow, which is joy's disguise ;

Assumed, to guide us to the skies :

Thrown off when there, as needed not,

Where consciousness of grief's forgot ;

Or to be thought of but as gleam

Of lightning, threatening in a dream,

Which rouses from a fear-fraught sleep ;

To make the heart with gladness leap,

That it was *but* a dream did scare ;

And God and *safety's* everywhere !

II. Occasional Poems.

THE EVE OF THE BIRTHDAY.

Lo ! on the threshold of another year,

    Thou standest, like a conqueror elate ;

Whilst I, with timid and prophetic fear,

    Predict the evils of thy lengthened date.

Like to a seer, do I plunge mine eye

    Into the dimness of each coming hour ;

To mark the tempest gathering in the sky,

    Which o'er thy pathway will portentous lower.—

Oh ! if for thee immunity from ill

    My prayers could purchase, how unceasing they !—

How should you angels marvel at the will

    Which grew in *strength*, the more that I did pray!

THE EVE OF THE BIRTHDAY.

Hope forward rushes; and, with hurried pace,

   Speeds to the goal, some promised joy that brings:

But fear the past more slowly doth retrace,

   And o'er the present broods, with drooping wings.

Hope grasps the future; but the substance shrinks

   Into a spectral shadow, when embraced;

As the feigned waters, which the pilgrim drinks,

   Sinks in the mirage of the desert's waste.

How fortune-favoured, could I but avert

   The disappointments thronging thee around;

But, as forbidden, oh, be thou alert

   To gain the wisdom in experience found;

Which doth instruct, that suffering must be

   The penalty exacted from mankind;

Light be the burden, which it lays on thee!—

   And prompt the aid, that thou for it shalt find!

Rejoice TO BE, though life, alas! is fraught

   With sorrows, which obscure its brightest sun;

It hath *one* gladness, which thine, sure, hath

   caught:

For by each breast the glorious prize is won.—

    Love! SENTIENT love! which life to feeling wakes

      From inert slumber, and from inert dream;

And on the soul in glowing lustre breaks,

      As if young seraphs spread supernal beam;

I do rejoice THOU ART.   Dear Heaven, be praised;

      Thanks, gentle planet, for the boon of life,

Which hath my sadder being often raised

      Above the veil of many a cruel strife!

Before we met, earth was a wilderness,

      With each emotion, like a captive, gyved;

But since, O since, it hath been little less,

      For my full soul, than Paradise revived!—

It was thy hand unloosed my slavish bonds;

      It was thy smile which set my spirit free;

How then my HEART unto my TONGUE responds,

      When asking God's most choicest gifts for thee,

They *only* know, who midnight pillows steep

      In tears of agony, no sobs betray;

How mournful is the memory they keep

 Of some fond trust, which time hath borne away !

How to the fair delusion the heart clings,

 So cherished as a truth, so treasured there ;

Though every passing moment deeper wrings

 The heart, a fallacy could so ensnare !

When He, who bids the " weary come and rest,"

 Invites me to this beatific sphere ;

When all the expectations of this breast

 In their true nothingness shall then appear ;

When my plumed spirit, panting to depart,

 But lingers still in company with thine,

The tenderness shall yet subdue my heart,

 Which, through death's changes, it could not
  resign.

Then, then, when watchers catch my final sigh,

 In softest whisper they shall hear THY name ;

The LAST on earth, the FIRST beyond the sky,

 Which could from me, BELOVED, affection claim !

REMORSE.

As one, his vision failing by degrees,

Consoles himself, the mist will soon disperse

Which seems to render all things indistinct,

And dims the lustre of the Orb of Day;

Until on him is forced the fatal truth,

That 'tis his *sight*, and *not* the skies are veiled;

So o'er my mental vision gathers mist,

Growing as dense as ever Blindness caused.

And one sole crime hath this dread darkness brought—

The crime, which made me prematurely old—

The crime, which mid-way in life's bold ascent

My steps arrested, bidding me return

Ere I had gained the Pisgah of my hopes,—

From whose exhilarating, breezy top

I might survey the Canaan of the heart,—

The Promised Land of Love, and that GREAT Joy,

(The young make breathless, even in idea,)

The full attainment of Ambition's dream.—

Panting and baffled, struggling in defeat,

Like gladiator from arena borne;

I did commence the slow descent which led

Into the valley of this death of shame;—

Heart-weary of a world I scarcely knew.

O awful is that withering of the soul,

Which parches into age its spring-tide bloom!

Awful to have its verdure blighted by

The simoom of remorse—its freshness turned

To aridness, as dry as desert-sands,

By the fierce blastings of its glowing grief!—

One who bestowed on me the fond belief

Of childhood's innocence, and woman's trust,—

I hurried to the grave in earliest prime;

Yet, not too soon, an angel to its God:

Save that, indeed, my hateful memory

May mar the bliss of Paradise for her,

Molesting it with earthly perfidy.—

Hence, hence, the tortures of my stricken breast!

Hence, hence, the anguish of my conscience torn!

Hence, hence, the desperation of my fears!

But, soft! but, soft! that which appeared Despair,

Dreary as starless sky 'neath Winter's night,

Hath changed to hope as bright as Summer's noon,

When cloudless radiance floods the azure dome,

At the glad thought of her great gentleness!

Oh! she will plead for me unto her God,

Yea, with an earnestness so powerful

As might seem wondrous, proving woman's love,

In its forgiveness, parallels His own,

When Wrong doth challenge its benignity.

And thus, through her whom I have most oppressed,

The amplest measure of redeeming grace

I shall receive, serene beatitude!

LONDON.

―――

"If any man speak, let him speak as the oracles of God."—
1 Peter iv. 11.

Fair Island, girdled by a mighty zone
Of cliffs precipitous, whose sharp ascent
Defiance frowns upon the ambitious foe ;—
With giant cestus belting thee around,
To keep at distance each approaching harm !—
Fair Island ! fair thy City of delights,
The envy, and the marvel of the world ;
The prosperous,—the erudite,—the great.—

Thou modern Rome ! Magnificent as was
The ancient empire, when the Cæsars reigned,

And pride and luxury dominion shared,

And arrogance attained the giddy height

From which it toppled down, no more to rise!—

Lo! equal pride and luxury are thine—

Lo! equal arrogance has dizzy grown—

Lo! equal crime precipitates thy doom,

Metropolis of grandeur, and of guilt,

Reeling beneath the vertigo of sin,

Yet *unaware* of danger neighbouring thee!—

Thy days are numbered,—on thy palace-walls

The same denunciation is inscribed

As seared the vision of Assyria's king;

Who gazed himself to blindness, when the words

Of fiery indignation smote his sight,

Which told that the *Invisible* was there,

To wrest the sceptre from his impious grasp.

Unmasked by the irreverent throng, who crowd

Thy busy thoroughfares, a Prophet walks,

Crying to the regardless multitudes,

" Woe, woe to the inhabitants of earth !

Woe, woe to ye who sleep, while broods the storm !

Woe, woe to ye who build in every street,

Yet set no watchmen on your citadels,

To warn of Death, who cometh like a thief,

When the night-hush is on the universe !

Woe, woe to ye whom pleasure enervates,

Whom splendour dazzles, and whom station charms!

Woe ; woe to ye the haughty, and the vain,

The self-exalted, and the self-esteemed,

Who set the foot upon your fellow's neck ;

And spurn whom God did mould from the SAME clay.

Woe, woe to ye who, lulled in soft repose,

And the voluptuous langour of your ease,

Forget, in the oblivion of the soul ;

From dust ye came, and shall to dust return !

Woe, woe to ye your Maker who bring down,

By your indifference, to the censure of

The TRULY suffering, and the FANCIED wronged;

Who feeling ye are blest above desert,

Look for prompt judgment on your thanklessness;

Conscious that God *must* be extreme to mark,

If He is just, your base ingratitude,

And them reward out of your forfeitures!

Woe, woe to ye who treat as madman's dream

The dread predictions, any instant may,

To your amazing horror, verify!

—Till, from its verdant valleys, rose on high

The purple column of sulphureous smoke,

Who credited Gomorrah was in flames,

Though angels came its threatened fall to tell?

Sodom! thou·fairest city of the plain!

The dance, the feast, the revel still was held

Within thy spacious chambers, till, appalled

By the hot thunderbolts from Heaven which fell,

The guests affrighted sought some means to fly,

And sank expiring on thy marble courts,

Black, suffocate, o'ertaken by swift doom!

And who will now believe this our report?

Who will attend the oracle divine

By wisdom uttered, timely caution teaching,

Until too late His vengeance to avert?

No ear will listen, and no heart will quail—

No hand in supplication be upraised—

No knee in prayer of solemn import bow.

The sons of Wealth, absorbed in sensual joy,

With senses blunted, and with reason dimmed,

See not the menacings His lightnings bear;

So leave their God, in irreligious scorn,

To smile and spare not: while the squalid poor

Think it is useless to implore His aid

Who never found their by-ways of despair,

But them abandoned to the penury

Which claims no thankfulness, and wakes no praise.

And thus each class, the mighty and the mean,

Resigns, to the fierce scathings of His rage,

The gorgeous palaces, the temples grand,—

And the low dens, the alleys, and the lanes,

Where sad, unthought-of poverty conceals

Its fever, and its famine, rags and shame.

Nor tower, nor steeple, nor the gilded spire,

Remains to glitter in the morning ray

Of that *calm* sun, which, from the placid skies,

Looks down serenely on the shaken earth,

To mark the site of the once beautiful,

And show that LONDON* hath become the PAST ;—

Another record for Tradition's page—

Another emblem of the Mutable—

Another extract from the Book of Time—

Another witness for the Mighty One

Who wrote " I am" upon creation's dawn,

---

* " The time shall come when a New Zealander, sitting on the broken arches of London-bridge, shall mourn for England's departed grandeur."—LORD MACAULAY.

And who will write "I am," at the Last Day,

The sole Eternal, Time and Death survives.

Bow down in awe, "O ye of little faith,"

And own the Infinite Himself reveals!—

For countless centuries, the desert-sands

Had curtained Nineveh, to cover up

Her glory, and her crime, until her name

Had almost ceased among remembered things.

But, in the age of rankest heresy,

When Scepticism ruleth paramount,

And Piety is driven from our fanes;

From Palestine's to England's favoured shores,

The hallowed relics are triumphant borne,

To show to Doubt, the Eternal, at its fall,

Decreed its resurrection at this hour,

To testify of Him, ye would deny,

But for the stones, which thus enforce conviction;

And your reluctant worshippings compel.

So, from Time's teeming womb, in lapsing years,

Another Layard shall, by Providence,

Be led to disinter the buried pomp

Of this still crescent, huge metropolis, ·

To find upon her charred and blackened stones,

The like inscription—" God, the Powerful,

Beholding the iniquity of Man,

And the sad groanings of the land, through sin,

The livid lightnings of His anger shot

From burning clouds, that city to consume,

Which held divided interest with Him ;   .

And, as in STRENGTH, so in PROFANENESS grew."

OH! TELL ME WHERE THE WEARY ARE AT REST.

OH! tell me where the weary are at rest?

Earth's fainting pilgrims,—where find they repose?

Upon Affection's sympathetic breast?

Within the grave, at Sorrow's final close?

The heart may ache,—but, if the heart be YOUNG,

It would delay to have Death's requiem sung!

Oh! tell me where the weary are at rest?

A seraphim, from the abodes of peace;

By Mercy missioned, did it come in quest

Of suffering hearts, to bid their anguish cease;

Lo! still enchained below, by some FOND tie,

Amid despair, they'd hesitate to die!

Oh! tell me where the weary are at rest?

   A maiden, pure as lily in its dell,

With one coy thought, scarce in her prayers confest,

   Though chaste as Innocence aloud might tell,

Can, on her bosom, yield a rest as sweet

For love, as Heaven's, when TEARLESS eyelids meet!

Oh! tell me where the weary are at rest?

   But low as whisper, angels hear alone;

For it would jar upon the soul opprest,

   If happier creatures caught the welcome tone:

For soft as prayers o'er dying babe should be

The quiet utterings of eternity!

GOOD NIGHT, MY CHILD!

"GOOD night, my child !"—Is the night GOOD,
That wraps us in its gloom to brood
O'er anguish, no cessation knows;
Which still weeps on, when eyelids close
In slumber, that should grant reprieve
To those, at least, who ONLY wake to grieve?

My mother sleeps.—"Good night, my child!"
Her lips *could* say—and—how they smiled!
Not in derision, but delight—
To thee, a thousand times, "Good night,"
Dear mother, who couldst smile on me;
Mid the afflictions pressing sore on thee!

My mother sleeps—my mother dreams—

May she have those celestial gleams

Of ecstacy, which fill the breast,

In the short intervals of rest,

When quiet is that active woe,

Which frenzies the poor brain with ceaseless throe.

She sleeps—my blessed mother sleeps !

Her sole release from want, which keeps

A watch, whose vigilance distracts

The brain it wears—the heart it racks.

My heart is OLD—Time's furrows there

Have been forestalled, by the rude plough of care.

I am so poor, that sympathy,

Emotion is too RICH for me !—

So poor—they'd mock, should I forego

My sorrow, for another's woe ;

And who'd the barren boon receive,

Which them occasioned not the less to grieve ?

Yet—could my heart's spontaneousness
More than mere sympathy profess;
Like Queen of Sheba—from the isles,
Where perfumed sunshine ever smiles,
I'd come, full-fraught, but not to them,
Bowed 'neath the weight of regal diadem.—

I'd come, full-fraught, but not to kings,—
But to those more neglected things
Whom Fortune never seeks,—who shed,
With breaking heart, and throbbing head,
The ebbless tears, whose confluent tide
The narrow strait of joy doth ne'er divide.

Oh! shall I never know THAT bliss,
(Supremest in a world like this,)
Such tears, in their sad course, to check,
And the wan lips in smiles to deck,
Which have not smiled since infancy,
And *then* on breast of misery?—

Once in a fever—or a dream—
I know not which—but I did seem
To have the gracious power, and will,
My soul's deep yearnings to fulfil;
Removing from each burthened breast
The load of agony, which so opprest.—

But never, in one CONSCIOUS hour,
Have I possessed such heavenly power;
I can but shudder, as I see
The HUDDLED groups of penury
In corners crouching.—Doth God's eye,
In such forsaken corners ever pry?—

Yes!—the Omniscient seeth all.—
On me, O God! let that eye fall,
Watching a mother while she sleeps;
To kiss away the tears she weeps:
And praying Thee, of Hope one proof
To send beneath this HOPELESS roof.—

Oh! when she wakes, that I *could* say,

" Dear mother mine, to thee, ' Good-day!' "

Yet—could she say to me—" Good night !"

In her most miserable plight ;

Her patience chides me—pardon, Lord—

Thou, even now, dost aid afford.—

Oh! it is Thou inspirest me,

To have a firmer trust in Thee !

Oh! nothing more that faith shall shake!

Dear, dearest mother, wake—O wake,

That we may bid the Heavens " Good day :"

Dawning on us, with more refulgent ray !

HEAVEN'S PERFECT CHRYSOLITE.

THE throne on which, with glory crowned,
  Transcendent Glory knew His own ;
Which myriad rays diffused around,
  Emitted from each costly stone ;
On which archangels trembling gazed,
  And seraphim approached with awe ;
Which with the blended brightness blazed,
  As once exalted prophet saw ;
God deemed a jewel far less clear,
  (Though dazzling its resplendency),
Than the rich splendour of the tear
  Which gems the eye of Charity.—

Such tear, an infant Rose once caught,
  (Expanding in the vernal morn ;)

Which she had wept, when over-fraught

With pity, for the fortune-shorn;

And sped it on a sunbeam, where

Cherubs earth's choicest gifts receive,

To treasure up, to witness bear

God doth not grief unsolaced leave;

For to a "perfect chrysolite,"

Heaven's chemistry transforms that tear;

That, RADIANT in Jehovah's sight,

Its gorgeous lustre might appear.

There's not a day—there's not an hour,

But from some eye such tear might flow;

Which grateful to Eternal Power

Would be as empyrean glow.

There's not a day—there's not an hour,

But hearts He animates to feel,

It is to HAVE a heavenly dower,

On misery to softly steal,

And, in His holy name, declare

    A truce to its wild war of woe;

And, with it, unreserved, to share

    The wealth, for THAT He did bestow.—

O think! how glorious 'tis to break

    The arrows of an adverse fate;

And let the wretched HERE partake

    Of bliss, all, ALL anticipate!

To trample on the barb, would rend

    The hapless breast, 'gainst which 'tis aimed;

Is, surely, to have reached the end

    Of Christian duty, which God claimed!—

O think! in corners most remote,

    (Ye, who have ne'er unprosperous been;)

His angels throng about, to note

    Where coy Compassion glides, unseen

By human pride, whose lofty looks

    Bend not to seek the hidden ways

Of sorrow, in the distant nooks,

    From which her practised step ne'er strays.

As One was speeding through the sky,

   Lo! on its rushing wings, it paused

To mark, in home of penury,

   That sudden plenty what had caused,

Amid the famished, shivering there,

   Solemn as spirits in conclave,

In accents, asking of despair,

   "When their's the rest would nothing crave?"

With what a transport of delight,

   One of God's missioned it beheld;

Who riveted the tearful sight:

   And the complaining bosom spelled;

Glad tiding breathing from the heart,

   In Pity's gentle undertone;

Which to the hopeless did impart

   The hope, they deemed for ever flown.—

Its radiant pathway through the sky,

   On swiftest wings, it did retrace;

To tell, to tell exultingly,

That a proscribed, degenerate race,

Did, God omnipotent ! retain

The Charity in Heaven was born;

Which, yet, at Sorrow's touching 'plain,

Which, yet, at sigh of the forlorn,

Buoyant, as moulted bird replumed,

For Woe's lone dwelling took its flight,

And, with its halo, re-illumed

The gloom of its pervading night ;

For well it knew the joy above,

The triumph Mercy would express ;

To learn that Pity, moved by Love,

The objects of acute distress

Made objects of unceasing care ;

Fulfilling thus Divine behest ;

Increasing, while it did NOT spare,

The portion, the Almighty blest.—

While Mercy of that Pity boasts,

On earth, O God ! abounding still,

Silence would hush the heavenly hosts

With ecstacy's unspoken thrill!—

The thrill, which never found a voice,

Save once, when choral hosts did sing,

" O Death, despair !   O Earth, rejoice !

Ye sin-redeemed, accept your King !"

CAPRICE.

So fair! so loved!—thy wayward mood,
    Is agony to me!—
'Tis worse than loneliest solitude,
    Companioned so by thee!
That solemn pause in sympathy,
    When the heart FEELS alone,
I *could* endure—(O misery!
    Such truth that I should own!)
But weary of continual taunt;
    O, would I could erase
The gentler words, my memory haunt;
    Which Love will there retrace.
I sped to thee, with such excess
    Of pleasure in my breast;

It still throbs with the happiness :

Checked—checked—before exprest.

'Tis ever thus—but let that pass.—

Mine's the intenser woe,

To love not less, alas ! alas !

The more thy faults I know.

Beauty's is not a tyrant's power,

(Invincible when meek) ;

It doth misuse its heavenly dower,

Which Love comes swift to seek,

When it its influence would test,

Its sway the more increase,

By deeming passion, ONCE confest,

Can never, NEVER cease,

Whatever the caprice it shows ;

Mistake of fancy born !

The love for tenderness which glows,

Chills 'neath the breath of scorn.

I do not hope thou wilt repent,

    Or grieve thou dost provoke;

So long as my mean neck is bent

    Submissive to thy yoke!

I've thought from thee to keep away,

    Thy beauty to resist;

And then I've thought how *long* the day,

    Ere came the hour of tryst.

Silence upon my soul might fall,

    Unbroken as the tomb's;

And muteness wrap, as in a pall,

    Each floweret there that blooms;

And darkness veil the sun, the moon,

    In awful mystery;

Within that soul could still be noon

    From thy refulgency.—

For I'd recal thy beaming look,

    When I my love avowed;

Which sparkled in the crystal brook,

 O'er which thy face was bowed;—

And softly to that soul I'd tell

 The whisper then I heard ;

Which from thy lips in music fell,

 As if a zephyr stirred

The chords of some Æolian lyre,

 Or baby fingers swept

The harp, a mother's hand did tire,

 To lull it till it slept.—

And then I'd think it was a dream,

 This sad reality ;

As woman, driven to extreme,

 Still generous must be.—

And then I'll think, thou didst but try

 To make me love thee more ;

Ah ! dearest ! let THIS satisfy :

 I only can ADORE.

COME BACK! BUT HASTE TO PARDON ME.

RETURN! thou Sabbath of my soul!—

Thy presence why so long delay?—

O come! the weakness to control,

Which that frail soul still leads astray;—

O come! with thy FIRM tone of prayer,

And ALL its turpitude declare.

Yet when on mine thine eye is bent,

Look then as He who passed not by

The world-deserted penitent,

In His celestial ministry;

Then, shall I feel, by THEE forgiven,

I may dare hope the same from Heaven.

The pang the most severe, which wrings

   The bosom of remorsefulness,.

Is that endured, when Memory brings,

   (Too late the evil to redress,)

The thought of one, intensely wronged :

With the DEAR worth to him belonged.

Alas! how little Vanity

   Doth e'er conceive, MUST come a time,

When it shall, in repentance, fly

   To him, so injured by the crime

Which love degraded—honour shamed,

Ere suffering its pride had tamed.—

Yet in the DARK hour Folly reaps,

   The heart for early love will crave ;

(The one pure pulse which still upleaps

   Above Pollution's turgid wave)

Nor dread repulse—nor aims mistook—

Nor scorn—which stronger nerves hath shook.

For God, to humble most that heart,

And it for Heaven to sanctify,

Doth the first love, which did impart

A foretaste of its ecstacy,

Re-kindle,—when contrition rends

The heart, self-love no more defends.

Yea—when this world the hardest goes

With those for it who've staked their all;

When cold contempt the first stone throws

At its poor martyrs, in their fall;

Then to that love the heart doth turn:

Which will not, out of pity, spurn.—

Oh! BUT for Pity now to sue!—

And fear lest it should be denied!—

O erring heart! thou well may'st rue

The blandishments of sinful pride,

Which made thee love esteem so small,

And gives such anguish to recall!

Ah ! what, save pride, doth now complain

   That pity is so mean a thing ?

The dove, that feels the arrow's pain,

   Can soar no more on buoyant wing,

Nor can, O Heart ! Love ever stoop

To her 'neath wounded fame doth droop.—

Love cannot love, without respect ;

   'Tis veneration forms its joy ;

When once on folly's ocean wrecked,

   Thou canst not back that love decoy ;

Sunk 'mid the waste of waters there,

It leaves thee, Heart ! to thy despair !—

Come then, as PITY, back to me,

   Let Mercy guide thee where I mourn ;

O come ! to set the spirit free,

   Of every earthly craving shorn ;

Save the insatiate desire

Thee to behold, and then expire!

YES.

Ah ! little word !—yet most potential thou,

To force the heart's best blood to flush the brow

Of manhood, with a pleasure palpable ;

Too quick for self-possession to repel !

Mine is now glowing,—sweet ! thine eye may see

The magic of that word of ecstacy !—

Mine is now glowing,—yet, I fain would turn,

To hide that wherewith it doth SEEM to burn,

Even from that eye, (thou dearest on the earth :)

Lest it should triumph, giving Rapture birth !

How long I've sought that " Yes ;"—yet now I fear

The confirmation of my hopes to hear ;

And my heart trembles with confused delight,

Like hers, who hath, on some expectant night, .

Dared the ordeal of that public praise,

Which doth its idol, on the instant, raise

Upon a pinnacle, whose dizzy height

The veil of faintness spreads before the sight;

For there are some few feelings, choice as rare,

Which, though of happiness, give pain to bear.

Life hath no recollection of true bliss,

Anterior, my own beloved, to this!

Oblivion hath enshrouded meaner joys,

To leave to that, this hour intense, employs

All space, all scope, all margin of the mind,

That atoms of beatitude, combined,

May form one gem unparalleled, for me;

Whose value yet is all derived from thee!—

How bright my future path, for rays divine,

Lo! from that HEART-set gem, on it will shine!

How bright my FUTURE path, by thee so made!—

Oh! for that "Yes," art thou not well repaid?—

Yet, yet, how long didst thou withhold from me

That attestation of felicity!—

Woman thus ever seeketh to enhance

The ecstacy, doth every sense entrance,

By coy delay; yet, if she could but guess

The torture she inflicts,—prompt to confess,

As Mercy, would she be her hidden love :

As BOTH are emanations from above.

——Silence in heaven once was : could it be when

The angels heard, what was concealed from men,

The low-breathed whisper,—faltered in a tone

So musical, 'twas fit for heaven alone,—

Of that soft " Yes," which did, in sooth, allay

The irritation of thy long delay ?

The " Yes," thou'st spoken, and canst not retract,

The " YES," so long my doubting soul which racked.

THE DYING HUSBAND.

LET my cool hand o'ershade those burning eyes,

    Which look so glowing in their watchfulness ;—

Who are they seeking for ?—Arise, arise,

    Calm vision, down those pain-propped lids to press:

That, in some healthful dream, disease may fade,

And my beloved awake, like man new-made.

Patience, my heart ! he'll wake, like man NEW made,

    But not for human hope, or misery ;—

But in those realms, where nothing can degrade

    Heaven's heir immortal, crowned with dignity ;—

When he hath paid, by suffering, the toll,

Those Paradisean gates admit his soul.

I miss the glad and gratifying tones,

   Which greeted me, when Love was in its Spring ;

Then, I shall miss the agonizing groans

   Which now, for thee, my melting bosom wring ;

And in the consciousness thou art at rest,

Command Despair to quit my hopeless breast.

Then, I shall miss the wishful, anxious eye,

   Bent, with such mournful interest, on my face ;

As if thou pitied'st me, that thou MUST die,

   And leave me here, with none to fill thy place ;

Yet shall I joy that thou no more canst be

Disquieted in spirit, EVEN for me.

Then, I shall miss the light,—the languid tread ;

   What is there not, I shall not miss in thee ?—

Oh ! I shall miss the world, when thou art dead,

   The world,—so verdant in felicity !—

Transformed to barren waste, whose ONLY green

Will be the grave, where thou art laid serene.

O restless Death !—why wilt thou slumber not ?

My senses ache,—to think how long since thine

Have, in a happy sleep, the pangs forgot,

Which shake thee so, our union to untwine ;

Our hearts' selection,—when love doth insist

To lead the judgment, whither it may list.

Art yearning for thy babes ?—oh ! let them sleep!—

They've watched with me, till feeling's self is dead ;

Oh ! let them sleep !—enough for me to keep

Grief's lonelier watch and ward, by thee, instead ;

They are too young, to witness scene so dire :

Why should they watch their slowly-dying sire ?

When all is over—my expressive tears,

Will challenge them to SYMPATHETIC grief ;

And then will Death, which, at the first, appears

A thing TOO undefined for youth's belief,

Be offered to the sudden hand-veiled eye,

In all its stark, and dread reality.

Thy blessing leave with me ; as HOLIEST trust,

    They shall receive it, and thy kiss also ;

Their artless prayers for it shall thank thy dust,

    And soothe thy HOVERING spirit's pensive woe ;

Shewing the little band, bereft thine aid,

A shrine for worship of thy ASHES made !—

Life's light's expiring ; lo ! as the fair morn

    Is breaking brightly in the orient,

To usher in a day, for me, but born

    To see the anguish, long, long, heart up-pent ;

Alas ! the same will not EACH day behold ;

Till, till thy grave this senseless form enfold ?

Hark ! merry voices smite upon mine ear !—

    Hark ! little feet are rushing to this room !—

I must prepare OUR babes—(farewell, most dear !)—

    UNSCARED, to enter in this senseless gloom ;

For they've just risen from that gorgeous dream

Which on the sleep of innocence doth beam !

FAREWELL.

'Tɪs not to pain thy heart, but ease my own,

That I address these final lines to thee;

For shouldst thou leave,—nor my regret be known,—

That heart would burst, with o'erfraught agony.

It is in vain to struggle to forget,

It is in vain to hope from Time relief;

For on my soul is thy remembrance set:

For my eternal adoration—GRIEF.

When I recal, (alas! when do I not?)

The proofs of love I have received from thee;

I consecrate with tears each blissful spot,

Endeared, nay, HALLOWED by their memory.

Go where thou wilt, sacred as saint enshrined,

  Thou'lt be to me, through every changing scene ;

While Thought pursuing swifter than the wind,

  Shall mock the distance standing us between.

Oh ! could I the assurance but attain,

  That thou wert happy, though not so through

    me ;

I think, I should the fortitude regain,

  Would me enable to REJOICE for thee.

Clear skies may darken, and their sun grow dim,

  And Hope expand its wings, from them to fly ;

Still one peculiar star will shine for him,

  Whose path is followed by Love's watchful eye.

Farewell ! yet not for ever ! we must meet ;

  Hearts linked like ours Death cannot sever quite ;

O we shall meet again in that retreat

  Beyond the grave, so calm, so pure, so bright !

Farewell ! unruffled may Life's barque down glide,

  O'er the smooth waters of a tideless sea !—

Farewell, beloved ! though oceans may divide,

My prayers, my soul, my thoughts will be with
thee !

O Heaven benign ! I to Thy care commend,

One far more dear than mortal e'er should be ;

To hover o'er him, some sweet seraph send,

Whose tender lineaments REMIND of me !

THE STOLEN KISS.

LIKE quenching, at a sudden stepped-on rill,

The thirst created by the noon-tide heat,

Whose waters bubble o'er the mouth they fill,

And speed fresh strength to the heart's languid beat,

Was the cool kiss upon my cheek she laid,

(First pledge of love, which modesty did seal ;)

The while, affecting slumber, I betrayed

Her tip-toe softness near my couch to steal.

I longed to gaze upon her flushed-up face,

But set mine eyes as in unbroken rest ;

I longed to clasp her in a fond embrace,

But held mine arms, impassive, o'er my breast ;

I would not so her bashfulness have shamed,

    Nor forced her lily-coyness to unfold;

I ne'er exacted, though I might have claimed,

    Another kiss, to keep that one untold;

But treasured the sweet secret all mine own,

    For meditation's purer reverie;

To be mused on, when the DARK years were flown,

    Which leave less gracious things to memory.

THE FATAL BLOW.*

O MIND !—what sudden darkness shrouds the light,

Which rose resplendent from the gloom of night ;

To life illuminate ?—O spark from Him,

Supernal Godhead !—what could instant dim

The radiance of intelligence, which glowed

With brightness, heavenly attribute bestowed ?

What unforetold eclipse involved in shade

That which " man little less than angel made " ?

---

* One portrait is that of an Earl of Arundel, with his little son
beside him, whose face is marred by a wild idiotic stare. The story
goes that the Earl, in a fit of passion, struck the boy over the head.
The blow made his son a hopeless idiot; the father, in his deep
repentance, and as a warning to others, had four of these pictures
taken. He is painted with the stick in his hand with which he
struck the blow.—NEWSTEAD ABBEY.

Hastings and St. Leonard's News, September 5, 1856.

What prematurely quenched the beam divine?

This hand inhuman, God! this hand of mine!—

Oh! my precocious,—my excelling child,—

Who on the assassin of thy reason smiled;

The threat deriding, as I aimed the blow,

Prostrated thee, and "laid mine honour low;"

As if it seemed impossible to thee,

To credit such barbarity in me.

My smiling boy!—my boy, to smile no more!—

Whose gladness, richer than an Indian shore,

Did freight our hearts with joy ineffable.—

Oh! what blank horror on thy mother fell,

When, in a voice as humble as of prayer,

I did the forfeit of my soul declare!—

O fatal rage! thee, thee, an idiot left;

And me of earthly happiness bereft!—

Stunted alike in intellect and growth,

A thing to touch a stranger would be loth;

I see thee ever,—day and night the same:

My agony, reproach, my torture, shame.

Oh ! hath hell torments which can mine exceed ?

From which I pray, how vainly ! to be freed.

To lay the burthen of that conscience down ;

Which wreathes for me, indeed, a thorny crown.

Can I forget ?   O Madness ! seal my brain,

O let it not the memory retain

Of that one glance abhorrent, cast on me ;

The one of holier pity cast on thee :

When thy poor mother struggled—not to hate

The author of thy lamentable fate ;

And yet for thee commiseration felt,

As did to retributive anguish melt ;

How then she clasped thee, till thy blackened face

Told the convulsion of that strong embrace ;

How then she sobbed and shrieked, then silent grew,

And thee still closer to her bosom drew,

As if her life-long labour now must be

To wait, and watch, and minister to thee.—

That glance was all,—she did no more upbraid,

But my heart whispered what hers left unsaid ;

The condemnation, which condemneth me,

To my unutterable woe, I see,

In the most mournful eyes,—whose earnest look

Hath never once her hapless boy forsook,

Since, sullenly, I dragged him to the feet,

It was his wont so readily to meet.—

Since, like a criminal, I stood before

The unconscious victim, who could not deplore

His own calamity ;—his stricken brain,

Alike insensible to joy or pain ;

No throb of native pity e'er to feel

For her, whose grief to demons might appeal,—

For him, who quailed beneath the vacant eye

Devoid, alas ! of kindred sympathy.—

Thus both, thus both, from his remembrance swept,

His ill-starred doom without cessation wept ;

Yet, not together ;—lonely and apart,

We wept unsocial,—yet, we knew, would start

The simultaneous tears, did almost choke
The stifled breasts, their bitterness ne'er spoke.

Estranged, and distant ;—dried, for us, the source
Which freely flowed of mutual intercourse
For his dear well-being, whose awful plight
Hung like the mildew of pernicious blight
Over the fairest blossom of our lives.—
How, at that thought, my dulled remorse revives !—
That thought pursues me, like avenging fiend ;
Or like the lightning, when, with head unscreened,
I brave the blasting of the lurid blaze ;
Which yet disdains me from the earth to raze.—

That thought obtrudes upon my fitful sleep,
Me to awake,—for what ? to see her weep ;
To see her weep, whom I durst not console,
Whose bourne of bliss is but the grave's sad goal ;
Bowed to that grave,—she yet pathetic prays
To Heaven, still to prolong her weary days ;

That she may tend on him, whose passive state,

One gentle act cannot reciprocate ;

Who knows not love doth on his steps attend ;

Who knows not love each faculty doth lend

His mental inefficiency to aid ;

My ruined boy !—my wreck up-stranded laid !

What ! what reflection, for a heart so fond,

To be convinced, he never can respond

To all the lavish love so bounteous spent ;

A babe for ever !—purposeless intent !

A babe for ever !—no progression bland,

The infant mind to genially expand !—

A babe for ever !—even of instinct void,

A creature, once the laws had safe destroyed !—

Yet she, that lady, delicate of nerve,

Doth all the needs of absent reason serve

To him.   So violent his mood alarms

Myself and others ; but her patience charms

To newer trials,—and to newer straits ;

And never, mid o'erwhelming griefs, abates.—

All this *alone* she doth ;—and ne'er doth ask

Help, help from me ;—yet mine's the harder task

To feel so alien,—that she never flies

To me, in complicate extremities.—

No more with us as with most wedded pairs,

Whose love a jealous emulation bears,

Each hap to spare the other, seeming not

Aware the sacrifice, self so forgot.—

Dead in our bosoms lies the fervid fire

Of such a generous, and pure desire ;

Yet, yet how mine doth yearn again to be

Familiar, in our closely-joined degree ;

To hold communion, like those fast-bound friends,

Whom, God uniting,—Death apart but rends ;

But there's that herald, idiot son of mine,

To dash, and daunt the spirits, might incline

To reconcilement, in the sadder hour,

When sorrow doth resentment overpower.

To threaten judgment, Heaven might intermit,

If that his mother's still remained unknit

To the ferocious father's, who could smite,

(Yea, in his own felicity's despite,)

The soul of him whose glory might have shed

A halo round this seasons-waning head,

And lent a lambent lustre to a name,

The World may censure, and I must defame.—

His mother, every mournful musing hid,

She might have prayed for me, oh! sure she did!—

She might have pitied me, beholding how

I softly went, with earth down-seeking brow;

She might have pardoned me, that I shall know

In God's good time;—oh! let it, God, be so!—

There's not one pulse to pleasure could it move;

But how will it enhance my bliss above!—

Then, be the knowledge of that pardon sealed,

Meet but 'mid heavenly hosts to be revealed;

It being the divinest offering

Which human heart as sacrifice could bring;

God-ordered, God-accepted, boon sublime!

Doth cancel from the register of Time

Such turpitude as mine,—and welcome wins

From Saints, who weep o'er fallen Nature's sins.

With penitence, which ever comes too late,

I have engaged Art to perpetuate

The rending of the heart, which mine hath seen,

(With not one interval of calm between,)

Since, since this hand, (which should have withered

    then,)

Struck down my son; to warn my fellow-men

From yielding to the promptings of that rage,

Perpetual war with peace doth after wage.—

Yet, oh! what limner's skill could ever paint

That heart's contrition,—or its love's restraint?—

The one I may not show,—the other tell;

No, no, remorse, affection, I must quell.

Who would for my remorse feel sympathy?

Who with my tenderness would flattered be?

Not she, my wife, though her angelic mind,

For every sufferer can compassion find !

Not he, my son, a soulless tenement,

A shrineless temple, with its vail still rent ;

Enveloped in a fear-inspiring gloom,

Impenetrable as the night of doom !

Nor yet one OLD associate, nor friend,

I stand aloof from all, and lowly bend

Me to the destiny I did provoke,

Until the fetters of my crime be broke :

When Heaven the reason hath restored whose loss

Hath been my expiating, self-borne cross ;

When me my son doth once more recognize,

And my wife looks with unaverted eyes ;

When I may hope the mercy from the Lord,

Which to true penitence He doth accord ;

When I may claim my portion in that state,

Bought at a price He can but estimate !

Then may I cry aloud, " *exultemus !*

Let us praise Him, who so exalteth us !"

THE DEAD TAKE NOUGHT AWAY.

Ask not the just-stripped heart, which grieves
　With that absorbing agony
That Death occasions, that bereaves
　Of hope—of joy—of ecstacy—
Whether the dead with them take nought ?
　For then they seem all, all to take ;
Their very sepulchre, each thought
　Abode of nursing woe doth make.—
The memory, (whose quickened sense
　Restores, with such integrity,
Each trifle, held of worth immense,)
　Dwells with the dead—and misery—
The lingering regret—the pain—
　The void—their presence still doth crave ;
In hearts can ne'er be filled again :
　The dead bear with them to the grave.—

The midnight tears from eyes, which shun

    The radiance Day hath onward led ;

Towards that arid desert run,

    Made by the ashes of the dead.—

The low communings of the heart,

    Sorrow's pathetic rhapsody ;

With, with Distraction's wilder start—

    Call on the dead—and hope reply.—

But when the anguish is outworn,

    Whose fierceness rent the heart in twain ;

When Nature prostrate, and down borne,

    Doth scarcely consciousness retain ;

When, when the frenzy of Despair

    Hath melted into tenderness ;

And hand of Mercy is seen where

    Seemed one empowered but to distress ;

Then, ask them what the dead possess

    Of Earth's accumulated store ?

(The smallest atom is not less

    Than that which to the grave they bore !)

Then, thankfully their hearts will own,

(Attempered to submissive peace,)

The dead belong to Heaven alone :

    With them, all earthly interests cease.—

That they take nothing to the grave,

    That they all earthly things reject ;

Nor wish of earth one boon to save ;

    Glad to escape from earth's neglect.—

That they are past all suffering now,

    All human error—human dread ;

The brand of Cain from off their brow

    God, God erasing—there to shed

The halo of that Glory's light,

    Which stars reflect through skies serene ;

To show the dead, in regions bright,

    Need nothing of this dim terrene.—

That the great penalty is paid,

    And cancelled sin's exacted due ;

And that the doom on mortal laid,

    The Immortal never more shall rue.

THE LAST.

FAREWELL, for ever !—quit me, to receive

The bought caresses which will beggar thee,

The sordid blandishments which but deceive

With simulations of Love's ecstasy.

Farewell, for ever ! though thy heart is steeled

Against me, with resentful enmity ;

Because to sophistry I would not yield :

I'll not conceal that mine's unchanged to thee.

Farewell, for EVER ! how my heart contracts,

Beneath the sudden spasm of despair !—

Yet, when the torturer severest racks,

The frame exhausted hath less time to bear,

H

And yet I seem, as in a wildering dream,

   It is so strange to think thou couldst depart ;

Me, me abandoning, without one gleam

   Of joy to light my isolated heart.—

That heart's a sepulchre of many tombs,

   (Of mouldering ashes, and of fresh decay ;)

While death's o'ershading pall eternal glooms

   The orient lustre of life's rising day.—

For, one by one, my buried hopes lie there,

   The hopes which came, as whisperings from the
      spheres ;

Like angel measures fondly that declare

   The tidings that the heart so gladly hears.

Hath my mistrust outworn thy love for me ?

   Oh ! have I judged thee wrongfully at last ?

Thou who for years, long years, couldst steadfast
      be,

   Canst thou my memory date as of the past ?

Forgive! ah! woman! apt thyself to blame,

To load thy guileless breast with faults unknown!

Did he not unto thee another name?

Has he not from thee to another flown?

Ah! add not the intolerable weight

Of self-reproach unto that burthened breast:

Thou art forsaken,—yield thee to thy fate:

There comes for such as thou a night of REST,

Hush, graceless Heart! wouldst thou thyself forswear?

If he be happy, thou in silence break!

Was not his happiness thy only care?

Then bless the one his happiness doth make!

Pray for thy rival, that she constant prove,

Oh! ne'er may she avenge his wrong to thee;

(Poor Heart! poor Heart! such pity now doth move:)

But spare him from the pangs of perfidy!

STRUGGLE STILL.

———

Listless as man, alas! could be,
  Subdued to such extreme
Of unresisting apathy,—
  As doth all effort deem
Worse than the waste, an idle strain
  Of mind, subdued by spell;
To action I was roused again
  By force invisible.
It came like order from a king,
  Despotical of will;
Whose messenger to me did bring
  Command, to " struggle still;"

To " struggle still, despite of all :"

    Sovereign of heaven supreme !

If Thou from " burning bush " didst call,

    I did not see the gleam

Which testified my God was near,

    My failing strength to aid :—

Why should I struggle, I who fear

    No more to be betrayed

By any ill, could happen now ?—

    I who no good expect ?—

Who wear the brand upon my brow

    Of Misery's elect ?—

How that command my bosom shook,

    Almost with death at strife !—

Each panting pulse my heart forsook,

    Then bounded back to life.—

'Twas like loud clarion-trumpets' blast,

    To armies in the rear ;

'Twas like the splitting of mainmast,

    By tempests'-lightnings sheer ;

'Twas like the cannon's threat'ning boom,
   Vibrating on the air ;
'Twas like the final trump of doom :
   Imagined by despair.—
It shook me !—yet—how to obey
   Command, so like hope's fraud ?—
Thou who commandest teach the way,
   Thy servant listens, God !

Have I not struggled with each wave,
   That beat upon hope's shore ?
Thou, then Omnipotent ! must save :
   I cannot struggle more.—
Such struggling hath exhausted me,
   I sink in sight of land ;
And turn instinctively to Thee :
   To lead me to the strand,

Whose golden sands my weak eyes daze,
   (Their glitter is so bright) ;
Sparkling as life's rekindled rays,
   Just melting in death's night.—

Yet let me sink—for peace may be,

  Nay—some unguessed delights,

In the calm bottom of that sea,

  Whose ruffled surface frights.—

Delights, to such as me, unknown,

  Of race the most forlorn;

Creatures which on the world are thrown!—

  Why are such creatures born?

Why? for the gems to serve as foil,

  The prosperous to bedeck;

Worms, cast upon the common soil,

  For fortune's birds to peck?

No! no!—the rivets of the chain

  Of nature's gradient plan;

To render to each reason plain,

  God linketh man to man.

His rising—His descending scale,

  His justice strictly guides;

And the mete due will never fail

  Him who in Him confides.

I did despair ;—I hope once more :—

    He ever wins who tries ;

I yet may gain the golden shore,

    Which dazzled so mine eyes !—

I'll struggle still :—yet—would not reach

    An eminence too high ;

A lowly station best doth teach

    Immortal destiny ;

I'll struggle still :—my energies

    Are all renewed by Thee ;

Thou monarch !—looking from Thy skies,

    With piteous love, on me !

The mandate came from Thee alone :

    Thy messenger did bring

That order straightway from Thy throne :

    My God—my Saviour—King !

DEATH.

———

I STROVE to banish the dark thought ; it did my mind
    so scare,
It seemed beyond my moral strength, with courage to
    prepare ;
To quit a scene so pleasure-fraught, to leave all I held
    dear,—
The world, to stay which more enticed, as jealous
    death drew near,
The hopes, so flush of future bliss,—the cherished
    memories,
Which, like the scent of faded flowers, fresh trodden
    down, did rise,

To sicken with their fragrance faint, until the reeling
　　brain

Did ache with that intense regret, acutest of all
　　pain ;—

While thought on thought rolled on and on, as wave
　　succeedeth wave ;

And made my spirit more recoil from the repugnant
　　grave ;

But now that it hath really come, emotions rash are
　　hushed,

And schemes which stretched to unknown years
　　reprovingly are crushed ;

And I am sinking into rest, as with that lullaby

Which closes on the mother's breast the fevered
　　infant's eye.

It is so blest, to be released from the unequal strife,

Which doth declare to meek as I, " War to the very
　　knife."

There is such rude contention in this crowded world
of cares,
Where no one with his fellow man one social feeling
shares;
Where banners of factitious hope are waving in the
breeze,
To lure away from quietude,—earth's holy, soothing
ease.

Upon my hot and throbbing brow a cooling hand
seems laid,
And a voice of soft encouragement whispers, " Be not
afraid ;
Gather thy strength for one LAST leap; the chasm
yawneth wide,
But faith will thee enable still to gain the other
side."
I feel a lassitude creep on like pain's reluctant sleep,
Or for a grief o'er which the heart is too out-worn to
weep ;

While even to affection's tone my ear seems deaf to
    be·:
Oh! is this resignation, Lord? or, is it apathy?

That which of late so terrified appears like night's
    dark dream,
Retreating fast before the light of morning's orient
    beam;
And I can scarcely recollect the horrors me beset:
Sweet anodyne, in heaven distilled, so teaches to
    forget!
In the serene, sequestered way, leads to eternity,
No step of hurried rivalry appears to outstrip me;
Though thousands may be threading it, I seem to
    walk *alone*,
Slowly, with awe-retarded pace, towards the mercy
    throne.
I feel, O Lord, as if, indeed, "life's conflict now
    will cease,"
And that I am about to find that everlasting peace,

The strugglers of this world find not, but those who've
  fought that fight,
Proclaims them the true warriors of Thee, Thou Lord
  of Might.

PEACE IS PROCLAIMED.

WELCOME, as cooling draught to lips which burn

With fervid fever's heat, (forbidding smiles,)

Is the glad news, announcing the return

Of one whose absence of all joy beguiles

The minute-counting heart, which reckons more

By anguish, than by hours, the timeless stay

Of the long looked-for, who can but restore

Due measure to Love's miscomputed day.—

Oh ! when the heart is the sole dial-plate,

The evening sun of Time must overshade ;

How must it watch—how wait—ere it can date

The gracious hope, its setting hath conveyed

Unto that fond and fainting heart which droops

    Beneath the sickness of expectancy;

And "the thick-coming fancies" which, in troops,

    Seem marshalled on by adverse destiny.—

When sweet conviction had dispersed the dread,

    That heart which tortured worse than certain

    ill;

When the belief came flush on it instead,

    That Love its plight would happily fulfil;

When full fruition crowned the lingering hope;

    When to the heart, the pulsing heart was

    pressed;

When he'd escaped, where gory Death did grope

    For victims, 'mid the flaming ruins, dressed

In tenfold horror, as war's wanton rage

    Destruction hurled with fire, as well as sword;

When fiends, not men, alas! appeared to wage

    The bloodiest battle ever on record;

Thought me assured, he had escaped the grasp ;

   Thought me assured, from danger he was free ;

When him I held in such tenacious clasp,

   As bade defiance to mortality.—

But, soft :—pause, choking Heart, crush down thy
   swell.

What dream was thine ? what mockery of delight ?

   Canst thou proceed ? hast fortitude to tell,

How swift he faded from Love's doubting sight ?

   He had brought home the most pernicious seeds,

(Life to infect within his sluggish veins,)

   The fatal malady malaria breeds,

Which reeking rises from the festering plains,

   Obscenely strewed with the unburied dead,

Whose only tomb is in the vulture's breast ;

   While o'er their bleaching bones pale moonbeams
     shed

A holy light, to sanctify their rest.—

While their mourned dust the summer's sweetness
    spurns,
While their mourned bones the winter's tempest
    stains ;
Eternal love their memory in-urns,
    And sepulchres in thought their blest remains.

The secret pestilence, like Moloch-pyre,
    Offered my precious unto ravenous Death ;
And when as in a sleep he did expire,
    I almost died, from grief-suspended breath.—
Then all was o'er—that all, oh ! how it wrings
    The heart that's wounded past the hope of cure !—
The heart that unto desolation clings,
    And pleased to suffering doth itself inure !—
Soon on the stillness broke a lumbering sound,
    And busy voices, busy feet were heard ;
As if Volcano, in earth's deep profound,
    Was, for convulsed eruption, demon-stirred ;

And sullen knockings smote the startled ear,

   And then a silence, whose appalling hush

Confirmed imagination's awful fear,

   And sent the life-blood with impetuous rush

Prone from the heart, to flood the dizzy brain,

   Yet not to kill, but, duly to stagnate

The vital agony, whose poignant pain

   Renewed activity would aggravate.—

Then, like babe-whisper, came a gentler tone,

   And a hot tear my icy cheek bedewed ;

Whence I perceived that I was not alone,

   Although all sympathy I had eschewed ;

Officious still, it heard the hearse depart,

   Then let the sunshine in the curtained room ;

Then let the sunshine in my curtain'd heart,

   Wrapped in the darkness of a denser gloom ;

And bade me hope,—while slowly crept away

   The solemn hearse, my HOPE from me which bore !—

I knew how trite was all that it would say :

   So craved, in mercy, it would speak no more !

Love, in despair must leisure have to rave,

To grow familiar with its misery ;

To grow familiar with its idol's grave :

Ere it can grow resigned to Heaven's decree.

EARLY SPRING, AND EARLY LOVE.

THE old and ague-stricken sought the sun,

For the spring's currents and the winter's blasts

Commingled still, retarding summer's heat.—

Girls, whose untown-worn health defiant made

The frame, though fragile, 'gainst the Boreal breeze ;

And Boys, whose veins glowed with a warm delight,

And aspirations as yet undefined,

Sped to an antique wood for primroses,

And harebells, which to Nature offer up

Diurnal incense, from their secret dells ;

Like piety, by heaven alone observed.—

Through hesitation shy, and bashful pride,

One lagged behind, delaying to advance ;

Though he loved more than the boy-men who pressed

Intrusively on those wind-battling girls ;

And though white fingers, like a flash of light,

Enticed him on, half sportive, earnest half.

But then his love was yet a hidden thing ;

And he did shrink, lest, in revealing it,

He should expose to many bitter scorns

The thought his whole existence sanctified :

So, with a slower pace and sorrowful,

He followed in the buoyant giddy train.—

He heard her gay laugh, suddenly repressed,

As if she feared its heedlessness might wound

His not far-distant ear ;—and, lo ! he writhed

To think that the melodious symphonies

Of that checked joyousness should be disbursed

On inharmonious beings, who nor felt,

Nor melted at their snow-soft cadences.—

Oh the sick heart !—it needs as mild a clime

As the sick body, shivering with disease !—

His yearned for some soft, southern atmosphere,

Such as love makes, where jealousy is not ;

Its tepid balminess to rarefy.—

Unconsciously, from out that musing heart

Her name leaped to his lips, a kissing joy ;

And 'dewed his brow with bliss ineffable :—

And then, as if a hope was in the sound,

He bounded forward, with elastic step,—

And her beheld in pensive mood apart,

As waiting for the spirit that should give

The ecstasy intensified to hers,

Which mutual and congenial love bestows.—

They left the broadway to the frolic throng,

And plunged into a narrower, denser path ;

And sauntered on, with hand embracing hand :

And eyes that sought and shunned each other's
        face ;

With now and then a word abruptly spoke :

But, oh! the rapture in their silence sweet!—

They were the last, the hamlet found at eve,

And not a primrose, nor a harebell bore

The hand, too honest for such artifice;

While all their clusters boastfully displayed,

With embryo taunts upon their mocking tongues.—

But ere they could deride, her blushes craved

The mercy of their speechless sympathy;

While his beseeching eye conscious implored

Their silent pity for her modest shame,

And for a love too serious for their jest.—

So each respected, and so each rejoiced

In the sweet union, which, though untold,

All guessed now bound those twain in solemn

      bond;

(Praying that nothing might dissever them:)

And wreathed their harebells, and their primroses,

And, with a tearful eye, and trembling hand,

Entwined their brows, the newly-crowned of love.

For the INSTINCTIVE mystery was stirred

Within their bosoms, and they instant felt

Constrained to sadness, pleasanter than mirth ;

As if a prophecy were there fulfilled,

Long looked for, telling their own destiny !

THE MURDERER.

A GRACIOUS new-born babe,—he lay,—
   Like slumbering flower, in fragrant rest ;
While she, his mother, wiped away
   The tears, sprang from her soul, opprest
With the deep sense of what she owed
To God for blessing just bestowed.—

A fairer infant seldom met
   A mother's captivated eye ;
To make her instantly forget
   Her recent travail's agony ;
But, seeing what by it she'd gained,
Its lingering throes she now disdained.—

All rapture was,—and gratitude,

And full fruition of delight;

Each thought was banished, would obtrude

On pleasure's proud, imperious right;

Her heart its suffrage did demand

From heaven's benignant, bounteous hand.—

And did He grant,—that Providence

To whom she did, in trust, appeal,—

The prayer of earnestness intense,

Which her felicity should seal

With that duration, only He

The righteous guarantee could be.—

She so believed.—No doubt arose

To shake her confidence entire;

Her soul was lulled to that repose

Such confidence can but inspire;

She felt how firm in faith she stood,

And said, with Him, " That all was good."

Joy in thy babe;—dream out the dream,

Which hope and promise for thee weave;

Young mother! gilded by the gleam,

More gorgeous than an eastern eve;

The golden glory doth invest

The sanctuary of thy breast!—

Joy in thy babe; ere seasons steal

The innocence thy senses thrall,

And, mortal, thou art made to feel

Of mortal the predestined fall;

Thou rearing him in strength to grow

For guiltiness which time must show.—

Joy in thy babe;—ere come the fears

Which rise, like spectres, in the shade;

And, ripe in forfeitures, appears

The criminal that time hath made;

And thou dost shudder, that from thee

He drew sustained vitality.—

Joy in thy babe;—while he is thine,

　The present is thy triumph's hour;

As in a solemn fane, enshrine

　His pureness in thy bosom's bower;

As Samuel from a world of sin

Was shut the Holy Temple in.—

Joy in thy babe;—nor forward look,

　Yet ceaseless Heaven implore, for him;

His life is still an uncut book,

　With uncontaminated rim;

With angel-written title-page,

Devout perusal to engage.—

As o'er each leaf thine head shall bend,

　Though disbelieved, what words may scare!—

What ominous predictions rend

　The spirit, terror bids forbear!—

Predictions, mocked, as unfulfilled,

Yet with a truth-like tremor thrilled!—

The arms, which 'twined thy neck around,

The fingers with thy ringlets played,—

Shall, in those lurid leaves, be found

Red in the blood of friend betrayed ;*

The very arms upheld with thine,

In homage to a name Divine !

In weird sadness, then thou'lt sit,

With grim despair associate ;

Who to thy soul will closer knit

Each grief, makes thee most desolate !

And count upon thy prayer-worn beads,

Thy penances for his misdeeds.—

And strip the veil from off thine heart,

And show the Idol overthrown

Which thou didst worship, all apart

From Him who worship claims alone ;

* " It cuts me to the heart to think that I should be thought
guilty of such a crime, when the poor fellow was more like a brother to me than anything else."—THOMAS CHRISTOPHER WORRELL,
the Murderer of George Carter, at Erith.

Weekly News, Nov. 23, 1856.

Proving devotion such as thine

To Fetish-image did incline.—

Yet if a pardon could be won,

Which Mercy freely might endorse;

It should be for the love a son

Doth from a mother's heart enforce;*

A love too sacred,—too sublime,

To bear analogy with crime.—

* " A celebrated artist, in one of his rambles, met with the most beautiful child he had ever seen. 'I will paint the portrait of this child,' he said, 'and keep it for my own; for I may never look upon its like again.' He painted it, and when trouble came, and evil passions moved his spirit to rebel, he gazed upon the likeness of the boy, and passion fled, and holier thoughts entranced his soul. Years passed away, and at length, within a prison's walls, stretched upon a floor of stone, he sees a man stained with blood, with glaring eyes and haggard face, and with demoniac rage cursing himself and his fellow-beings, and blaspheming God as he lay waiting for the hour of his execution. The artist transferred his likeness also to canvas, and placed it opposite to the child's. How striking, how complete the contrast! The angel boy—the fiendish man! What must have been the feelings of the artist, when, upon inquiry, he ascertained that both the portraits he had made were of the same individual! The beautiful innocent child had grown into the hideous, sinful man."

The Weekly Times, December 28, 1856.

And, in his love-deserted cell,

(The hooted of the common cry ;)

In late remorse, will he not dwell

On his fond mother's gentle eye ?

On his fond mother's smile, which came

Whene'er (how oft !) she blessed his name ?

The eye, down flooding rapture's light,

The smile, sought seraph's sympathy ;

Shall at the aspect ne'er grow bright,

Denounced to public infamy ;

The mob-reviled—the mob-pursued,—

The wretch, with guilty blood imbued.—-

Yes—in his felon-cell, shall steal

The moaning of her misery :*

* " But who can describe the heart-rending scene that ensued :
the anguish of the aged mother, as she prayed to God in broken
accents to give her strength in that trying hour, and the wild unutterable looks of the condemned murderer as he gazed upon his
unhappy parent, made wretched by his wickedness ?

" Tears rolled down her furrowed cheeks, and her full affection-

And dream of infancy reveal

His mother, as if kneeling by;

And he shall wake, and find her there,

That mother, with her pardoning prayer.—

What crime a mother's love can bar?

What shame prevent a mother's tears?

Oh! that is like the Polar-star,

Which never from its circuit veers;

But shineth on, as it hath shone

Since first Heaven's orbs to man were known.

Though but a dream the mother dreams,

Though but the merest phantasy;

They are like the precursor streams

Of lightning, sweeping o'er the sky;

ate heart seemed as if it would burst before she was able to express
her concern for her unhappy son, and to assure him that, although
he had cruelly violated the ties of humanity, and all that is dear in
this world, she still felt a mother's love towards him."—THE EXE-
CUTION OF CASTLE, AT BEDFORD, FOR THE MURDER OF HIS WIFE.
                                    Daily Telegraph, April 2, 1860.

Which tell the storm is gathering fast,
To ride destructive on the blast.

Though but a dream, in fitful sleep,
    Depicts that mother to that son;
Lo! he shall wake to see her weep,
    For trespasses which he hath done;
To feel her hot, impassioned tear,
A heated brand, his brow to sere.—

The little mounds,—the infants' graves,—
    The fairy hillocks, churchyards dot;
Affection's dearest thought, which craves,
    As its love-consecrated spot,
The Ark of spotless purity,
Oasis of the memory.—

Yet mothers there will vigils hold,
    And " sorrow without hope" o'er them;
Oh! let them be, by cherub told,
    Their babes, crowned with Heaven's diadem,

Rejoice at being safe from harm,

And bland seduction's fatal charm.

The mother,—once of him so proud,

The gracious new-born babe,—whose fate

The sombre mystery did shroud ;

The Poet's mind did penetrate :

Her life had spent in thankful prayer,

Had grave of childhood been his share.

When, in his manhood's prime, she found,

How prone to err his course would be ;

Until in manacles were bound

The arms, she deemed as virtue's free ;

The babe such attributes displayed,

She marvelled for what more she prayed.

The daisies will refuse to braid

His grave of ignominious shame ;

And old and young recoil, afraid,

From the dark shadow of his name ;

Yet pause compassionate to gaze

On the wan woman there who stays.

True to her mother's instincts, she

    That dreaded grave will ne'er forsake ;

Undaunted by the obloquy

    A landmark of it scorn doth make ;

Like tabernacle in the waste,

To it, in each extreme, she'll haste.—

Until the hours ring out her date

    Of suffering, and thwarted joy :

And she is summoned to that state

    Of bliss, above all earth's annoy ;

Where cancelled is from memory

Of sin atoned the PENALTY.

THE RETREAT OF THE RUSSIAN ARMY.*

THEY are retreating,—swift retreating ;—
The Lord is fighting,—He is beating
  Else indomitable foes ;
Still, in disorder, armies flying,
Trample on the dead,—the dying,—
  For whom earth in mourning goes.—

Still retreating,—cohorts calling
Wildly on comrades, spent,—and falling,—
  "Haste ! for Heaven is on their side !
Haste ! haste ! the God of battles, rising
In their defence, whom we despising,
  He hath forced His wrath to 'bide !—

* "The Russian army is retreating in confusion." (Turin
Paper.)—MORNING POST, Oct. 2, 1855.

British and French,—our powers out-daring,

Whom, He protecting, death is sparing,—

    While our slaughtered bar our way.—

Oh ! for one hour,—that same God aiding

Our laurels, 'neath their triumph fading,

    Would not victory crown our day ?—

Comrades ! farewell !—with thoughts despairing,

We are to our homes repairing ;

    (Homes of desolation,—gloom,—)

To hear your widows,—orphans raving,

Hapless,—hopeless,—mercy craving,

    To hasten on releasing doom !

Comrades ! farewell !—repose in glory ;

We but survive to tell the story

    Written in your wasted blood !

We are retreating,—YES ! retreating,—

Trembling at our foiled country's greeting ;

    For conquest ebbing at the flood !"

Yes ! they're retreating,—God be praised !

On every bastion will be raised

The flags of England, and of France,

And in the air will gaily dance.

No ! spread by pity, let them shroud

The naked dead, the plains which crowd ;

For valour, warm in victory,

Melts o'er its fallen enemy.—

Yes ! still retreating ;—those allies

Beheld with glad,—yet scorning eyes,

The frantic rush the Russians made,

To 'scape from whom they DID invade ;

And then a nobler feeling rose,

Within their bosoms for their foes ;

The victims of despotic sway :

The subjects born but to obey !—

Yes ! still retreating ;—sickening sight !

Oh ! how precipitate their flight !

No time allowed regretful heart

To show its agony, to part

With fortress deemed impregnable;

Till 'neath superior force it fell!—

No time, one backward look to cast

On glory, now for ever past!—

Yes! still retreating;—victory's voice,

Bidding, exulting hearts rejoice;

Is silenced as the strains arise,

Which to the God of Destinies*

Ascribe the honour of a fight,

Won only through His potent might;

And hymns and psalms the shouts succeed,

Which first announced the gallant deed.—

* "A Te Deum has been sung in the Cathedral of Sebastopol, in the presence of Marshal Pélissier. Another church is appropriated to the English."—MARSEILLES, 29th September, 1855.

Yes! still retreating ;—pause awhile,—

Hark! hark! within the hallowed pile,

By bigot left to ruthless flames,

The homage which the victor claims ;

And which, Sebastopol, thy shrine

Does consecrate, as fane divine !—

Pause, Gortschakoff !—then—sullen flee,

With slaves compelled to follow thee !—

Yes! still retreating !—dauntless brave,

Who slumber in your gory grave ;

Awake! and listen to the beat

Of that ignoble, base retreat !—

Hark! to the dull, continuous tread,

Which shakes the ground above your head ;

Then, sleep again ! your work is done ;

Young heroes ! deathless conquest won !—

Yes! still retreating ;—turn, and see,

The lurid flame's intensity ;

(Armies ! undisciplined that fly !)

Gleaming terrific o'er the sky !

And the remembrance of its glare,

To Russia's snow-girt regions bear ;

To lend an artificial glow,

To freezing narrative of woe !—

Thou ! by insane ambition led !

Thou Emperor, defeated,—*dead !*

Thou didst not hear the bubble burst,

Thine heart which so inflated—curst ;

Thou canst not know, the Lord hath made

A mockery of thy pride,—parade,—

Handful of execrated dust ;

In what a shadow didst thou trust !—

How oft must God example make

Of despots, for the oppresséd's sake ?—

How oft must. God the warning give,

Not for ambition monarchs live ?—

How oft must God be forced to smite

Injustice, in the cause of right ?—

How oft, O tyrant, must the Lord

Such overthrow as *thine* record ?

STAR OF THE NORTH IN GLOOM THAT SETS.*

BUT yesterday, and thousands bowed†

　To thy Imperial state ;

So vast,—thou couldst not count the crowd,

　That thronged thy palace-gate ;

Whom thou didst think thy native worth

　Assembled thee to praise ;

Alas ! the vanity of birth,

　How does it self upraise !

---

* The Emperor Nicholas of Russia.
† "But yesterday the word of Cæsar might
　Have stood against the world : now lies he there,
　And none so poor to do him reverence."
　　　　　SHAKESPEARE'S " JULIUS CÆSAR."

But yesterday, and thousands pressed

To gaze upon thy face;

And, with a servile fear, confessed

Thy power to grace *dis*grace;—

And crouched beneath the trampling foot,

And kissed the scourging hand;

Nor dared the rebel question put,

"Why God so scourged the land?"

Where, King! is that obsequious crowd,

The vassals of thy wealth?

Not thee approaching in thy shroud,

With sorrow's step of stealth;

But sped the rising sun to hail,

Thy setting renders bright;

While thou, death-quenched, must sudden pale

Thy "ineffectual light!"

Thou'st held thy temporary sway

O'er autocratic rights;

And now, deposed, thou makest way
   For him, new rule delights ;
Thou hast performed thy mimic part
   On Grandeur's gaudy stage ;
And Fortune now dismissed, thou art
   A Player, none engage !—

Mere semblance of investiture
   Not e'en canst thou bestow,
Upon one flatterer, to allure
   Him to remain,—for—lo !
As naked as from mother's womb,
   Monarch, thou must descend
To the humiliating tomb,
   Where mundane honours end.

The meanest may revile thy name,
   Nor tremble at thy frown ;
And, with long-nurtured hate, defame
   Thy idolized renown ;

And he, who quailed beneath thine eye,
　　May, with uncovered head,
Unawed, to thy remains draw nigh,
　　And scowl upon the dead.—

Nor rank, nor riches, purchase love,
　　Nor gild a Tyrant's cause ;
The mercenary they but move
　　To venial applause.
For minds of nobler stamp despise
　　External attributes ;
And what the vulgar eulogize
　　Consider but imbrutes.

But equal all by death are made,
　　When man to dust returns ;
The beggar, of the king afraid ;
　　The king, the beggar spurns :

The outcast, and the courtly-bred,

(At one tribunal tried,)

Shall, in the Session of the Dead,

Be simply classified !

Ah ! tears were shed, though not for thee ;

Tears of heart-wrung despair ;

When multitudes, in agony,

Did to one spot repair

To recognise the mangled,—maimed,—

The dying,—and the dead,—

The fragments which affection claimed :

Objects of love and—dread !

While Superstition's wizard aid,

Sent frenzy prescient sight ;*

* "The celebrated great bell, 'Reni,' suspended in the tower of St. Ivan in the Kremlin, whilst being tolled for the Emperor Nicholas, fell in consequence of the iron supporters giving way, and broke through three separate stories of vaults, killing five persons on the spot, whilst five were wounded severely, and four slightly. The accident made a deep impression at the time on the

Whose threats prophetical delayed

Thy spirit's hurried flight;

To learn the dire calamity,

Thy subjects filled with woe,

Did, for thy great iniquity,

God's judgment doom foreshow;—

For war, thy rash ambition waged,

The war of stubborn pride;

Which with a slaughterous fury raged,

And loud for vengeance cried;

The war, denounced by God, and man,

Whose end thou ne'er shouldst see;*

Which they did stigmatize with ban

Of blood-stained infamy!—

minds of the superstitious Russians, who regarded it as a direct
visitation from heaven in condemnation of a war undertaken by
the Emperor; and processions were made, fasts instituted, and
candles burned to the Panagia, or Holy Virgin, to appease the
wrath of heaven."—THE NEWS OF THE WORLD, July 15, 1855.

* "The Emperor Nicholas of Russia died March 2, 1855. The
fall of Sebastopol, and the retreat of the Russians, Sept. 8, 1855."

Wild shrieks of anguish pierce the sky,

   As "passing-bell" was tolled

For thee whose awful destiny

   Eternity enrolled

Among the fiat-verdicts passed

   Upon the summoned *there ;*

Thou! whose triumphant reign, at last,

   Ends like a breath of air !—

O pride of station !—held in pawn,

   (The pledge, Death shall redeem ;)

What art thou, when God hath withdrawn

   His transitory beam ?—

A comet, that hath sunk in gloom ;

   A flash, that dazed the eyes ;

The phosphorescence of the tomb,

   Doth from corruption rise !—

O pride of station !—strengthless power !

   Shadow of giant-might ;

L

Frailer than that fair tropic flower,

Counts being in one night;*

That man,—the Son of God,—the Heir,

Joint-heir with Christ,—(death-free;)

Should strive, with such life-wearing care,

After a shade like thee!

Instead of that inheritance,

(That Kingdom so secure;)

Beyond vicissitudes of chance;

Which must, for aye, endure!—

Which the Almighty grants to those,

Who, reigning here below,

Can, when He Emperors doth depose,

To Him rejoicing go!

O, Death man's fortitude does test,

As crucible fine gold;

* "Cereus grandiflorus."—GILBERT'S "WONDERS OF THE WORLD."

Stripping off titles, did invest

    With honours manifold ;

Precipitating, as base dross,

    The dignities so dear !—

Ah, happy he ! who counts no loss,

    What Death did not revere !—

Ah, happy ! when the kingly crown,

    (As burthen too long borne,)

World-wearied monarch can lay down ;

    Yet feel his brow unshorn ;—

Conscious, a costlier coronet,

    (By king-maker Divine,—)

Upon that Heaven-sealed brow is set,

    Beside the Lord's, to shine !

MY BABE.

FIRST vernal blossom of my wedded spring,

    Bright morning's flushings of its summer's noon!

Why art thou fading? what bleak wind can bring

    The freezing current, withers thee so soon?—

Where is thy fragrance? where thy vivid bloom?

    Thy sparkling eyes? their look of artless glee?

I cannot see them, in this darkened room :—

    Alas! what light could show them now to me?

How parched the little hand, in mine I hold,

    It burns to seething in my shuddering grasp;

Yet, lo! I tremble lest an icy cold

    Should chill to death the fingers I enclasp.

How groans my heart, at each sad moan of pain!

    O, would I could endure thy pangs for thee;

What torture, darling! would I not sustain,

  Couldst thou but only once more easy be?

Mine throbs to frenzy, as thy restless head,

  (Upon the pillow which I vainly smooth,)

Tosses impatiently, as sleep were fled

  For aye the couch it was so wont to soothe.

O thou! expiring even before mine eyes,

  Thou babe, who came, like Hope, to seek my

    breast;

Thou strickened loveliness, that prostrate lies:

  All earthly hope upon thee still doth rest!—

Yet that perplexed confusion of the brain,

  Proceeding from absorbing agony,

Forbids me, though I wish it, to explain;

  That my mute torture is not apathy.

Thy bed of suffering I sit beside,

  Unheeding hours which Time's progression

    strike;

While thoughts ungoverned wander far and wide:

  All filled with thee, and grief, yet none alike;—

The random sport of inconsistent Fear,

    Which vary but from anguish to regret;

And then return to anguish, while, with tear

    Of dread foreboding, my wan cheek is wet.

My beckoned cherub! Heaven-invited guest!

    While thou art here, while thou art spared to me;

Yea, after thou art gone, this yearning breast

    Will still bestow its every thought on thee!—

How all will mind me then, that once on earth

    I was the favoured mother of a child,

Brought such abundant blessings with its birth,

    That I the fortunate of Heaven was styled.—

Oh! then will Envy, sickened at my joy,

    Melt in compassion at my rapt amaze;

That God, so gracious, could a babe destroy,

    He made so worthy of a mother's praise.—

But froward apprehension, wait, oh, wait!

    Thou still art living, Sweet! thou art not dead!

Then let me not the ill anticipate,

    From Terror's false prediction haply bred.—

The reed I lean on droopeth to the stream,

  Bowed, though not broken, by the tempest-blast ;

The ray I gaze on is a murky gleam,

  By that still lowering tempest overcast ;

That reed, to bear me up, doth stronger grow,

  Its pliant stem erect and firm appears ;

And, brightening through the storm, that gleam doth

    throw

  A radiance which the sky of Hope now clears ;

For the Unerring, who must needs be right,

  (Despite the sceptic's unbelieving scorn,)

Hath said, " Though sorrow may endure a night :

  Take heart, O Grief! joy cometh in the morn."—

And hath not mine, my babe, endured that night,

  Fighting for thee, with Death? but, in the East,

Is breaking now that morning's joyous light,

  Which shows my night of agony hath ceased.—

Which shows the battle ended, conflict o'er,

  That I may trust, that I may hope again ;

For He, Death's arbiter, can still restore,

  To Faith, the thread of life He cut in twain.—

A Lazarus He lifted from the grave!—

  A widow's son did He not too give back?

And I might have been sure, that He would

  save

  My son also, had not my faith grown slack!—

Oh! as its fire so kindles in my heart,

  So holy, fervent, its seraphic flame;

I feel, as " Mary chose the better part,"

  To God submitting, I could choose the same;

And almost give an angel unto Him,

  And thee secure His everlasting bliss;

Letting thee wing thy way beyond the rim

  Of such a sorrow-circling space as this ;

But Nature falters at the sacrifice,

  Weak, human nature, hesitating still

To win itself a passport to the skies;

  On earth fulfilling Heaven's benignant will ;

But He will pardon,—oh, He will forgive

Thy mother's wavering, and mercy stretch;

For, losing thee, He knoweth, while I live,

Pity will not condole a sadder wretch.—

Oh! He *hath* pardoned!—as I steadier gaze,

Returning life is spreading o'er thy cheek;

Let common joy express itself in praise:

My joy for this, O God, I cannot speak!

MY WASTED SPAN.

Oh! he who at the close of his spent years,

Indifferent to their futile course appears;

Who shrinks not from himself, nor from the eye

Of stern Omnipotence turns tremblingly;

That man is worthier pity, than the one

Who'd fain each erring action were undone:

For he, alarmed at consciousness of sin,

May, through remorse, its mitigation win;

But he, who quails not at iniquity,

Is *bad* to live,—but, oh, far *worse*—to die!—

My "three score years and ten," are they not run?—

And am I wiser than when they begun?

What have I learnt of the essential good,

Which, for Salvation, must be understood;

In all that precious time,—which, fleet as breath

Of morning-zephyr, wafted me to death?

How have I hunted after shadows vain,

The phantoms which the grasp could not retain,

But which eluded every fond desire,

And, like loved CHRISOM, did in birth expire!—

How have I followed that deluding Pride,

The mocking Anak, whose colossal stride

Did span the "Bridge of Sighs," which I must cross,

To reach the goal, whose vaunted prize was dross!

How have I thought that time was yet to spare,

Before such solemn aims need claim my care;

And dallied with the hours, and joked away

The moments leading to the Judgment Day!—

Yet I remember,—(and the pang of soul,

As of the past I read the shrivelled scroll;)—

How, on the threshold of life's promised date,

I did its several seasons calculate;

To bring forth fruits, whose garnerings should be

In the ripe gatherings of Eternity;

Yet barren rocks alone the seed received:

And not one full-eared harvest have I sheaved!

Now, now I feel the error of my ways,

Yet, like the culprit who from terror prays,

At "the eleventh hour," I bow the knee;

But from a God of Vengeance fain would flee;

Striving to flatter fear, to soothe despair:

By censuring the burthen all must bear;

And, with the sceptic's groundless sophistry,

Struggling accusing conscience to defy;

Whispering my stricken heart, "Could I the ban

  ban

Evade of Trespass?—Am I not a man?"—

Then, melting into penitential shame,

Not my Creator, but myself I blame;

And wish myself upon my mother's breast,

Her prayers for me still unto Heaven addrest.

To snatch me from Destruction's dark career ;

She died too soon, me leaving drifting here,

Like a dismantled bark, whose pilot fled,

When to the shore the startled seamen sped ;

When flaming lightnings rend the quivering skies ;

And, them to quench, huge surging billows rise ;

When Ocean is a monstrous catacomb,

And the heaped dead obtrude upon the home

Of the Leviathan, whose frothy breath

Enshrouds thy shroudless, thou immodest Death !

She died too soon ;—yet she may intercede !

Faith in a Mother's love is still the creed

Her prayers instil in the young, ductile mind,

Which hardened Age's doth, like treasure, find,

When beggared of all else, to cheer, and speed

The spirit on to a Diviner creed.

With heart as desert as that Arctic-waste,

From whose chill aspect vagrant sunbeams haste ;

And sullen vegetation, checked, and slow,

Refuses o'er its spectral plains to throw

The vivid mantle of its cheerful green ;

I unavailing mourn, that I have been.

It seems so terrible, to have no time,

The heights of Everlasting Life to climb ;

When Death is in the valley,—and the doom

Of Fate unchangeable is in the tomb !

THE VALLEY OF THE SHADOW OF DEATH.

"When the unclean spirit is gone out of a man, he walketh through dry places, seeking rest, and findeth none."—St. Matthew, c. 12, v. 43.

Grim, as the regions of the damned,

And fetid, as if over-crammed

With writhing beings, tortured by

Diseases of mortality,

Was the dark valley, where I found

Myself,—and horror most profound.

" There, one by one—then, two by two—

Of all the dead I ever knew,"*

Before me solemnly defiled;

Nor one among those spectres smiled,

* *Vide* Allingham's Poems.

As if was recognized a face,

Remembrance melted to retrace.—

And still each instant myriads sends,

(Oh ! have I lost so many friends ?)

And still each instant did restore

More wanderers, from the Stygian shore.

The young looked old as wrinkled age,

And all as if they'd died in rage ;

Resisting with defeated might,

The victor of unequal fight;

And concentrated strength did waste,

Like one, who climbs a hill in haste,

Spent long before the summit's gained,

Which by no effort is attained.

The sky, opaque as starless night,

Was yet streaked with sulphureous light ;

Enough to render visible

A scene that nought could parallel.

O Muteness !—Nature shrinks to bear,

Above—around—and everywhere—

Intolerable to sustain,

Relieved by shriek of human pain,

Relieved by human agony;

Though awful its blaspheming cry!

I trod upon the tangled brake,

Hoping to rouse the hissing snake

In torpor coiled,—abhorrent, till

That silence did with terror fill

My soul,—and made it almost cling

Familiarly to loathsome thing.

I strove myself to speak—to scream—

But, like the mockery of a dream,

The wildered senses which abuse,

Articulation did refuse

One demonstration clear to give,

That I, still in the flesh, did live,

More than the shadowy ghosts which went

There to and fro, with no intent.

M

The black forms of gigantic trees,

(Through which swept no refreshing breeze)

Calcined by scathing lightnings, aimed

To pierce that sky, whose air inflamed

Seemed heated from some furnace-glow;

Seething volcanic, deep below.

No bird—no flower—no herbage green—

Were in that desolation seen,

To break monotony as dread,

As could but be, where all was dead.

No sound—not one—the stifled breath

Was utterance—choked—where only Death

And Silence held supremest sway;

Nor Echo dared to disobey.

Tremendous hush !—O stillness !—Fear,

O'erwhelming found—longing to hear

The cataract's wild roar—the crash

Of thunders, as they furious dash

To atoms the thick clouds, and fray

A 'passage for the tempest's way !

Pressing against the shrivelled skin,

Yet rattling not the bones pent in

Their yellow-parchment prison-den :

The bones of once strong stalwart men !

Is there such silence in the grave ?

Oh ! do not there the desperate rave

O'er their lost souls, and try to rend

Their shroud-bands, and more freedom lend

To the brain's tension, which then seems

Bursting with woe that over-teems?

My own brain seemed so on the brink

Of madness, that I paused to think

Of childhood's hours—of childhood's bliss—

O God ! of anything save this !

Yet—yet in vain : the present scene

Would, with its horrors, intervene

Betwixt my memory—and my dread,

And direr agitation bred.

M 2

My blood-shot eyes still upward turned,

That with that scalding anguish burned

Which the Sahara's parching wind

Inflicts upon the traveller blind,

Straining through his galled lids, to mark

In the dull heavens one transient spark,

Struck from the Empyrean's blaze;

Whose fires the Seraphim upraise,

To show Eternal Light was where

God bade it be—to witness bear

That sun and moon did magnify

The everlasting Majesty;

And that the heavens' star-studded frame

Did, too, that majesty proclaim.*

Lo! while I looked—a ray of light,

Condensed from all that is most bright,

With dazzling lustre overspread

The lowering mass of clouds, and shed

---

* The heavens declare the glory of God: and the firmament
showeth His handy-work."—Psalm xix. 1.

Resplendence on them—till the eye

Quailed 'neath excess of brilliancy.*—

Another—and another came,

Rapid as chariot wheels on flame,

That for some guerdon fierce contend,

And last but till they gain their end.

Till the convex-like burnished shield

Of warrior glittered, and revealed

To my o'er-awed and baffled gaze

Sight which, in sooth, did vision daze;

Sight which no man can see and live!

To which no thought can language give!

While still those heavens did more expand,

Like sea, which so usurps the land,

That pilot this no more can trace.

As Paul, in terror, hid his face†

---

* "He saw; but, blasted with excess of light,
 Closed his eyes in endless night."—GRAY.
† Acts ix. 4.

From the insufferable light;

Blinding to unregenerate sight:

So I, down on my face did fall,

When from the heavens a voice did call,

Where only the Ineffable

Could, throned in native glory dwell;

" I am the Resurrection—Life;—

Look up! behold Creation rife

With unsurpassed magnificence;

With Godhead's high omniscience!"

Mysterious Heaven!—what change was
    there!

It to describe, may mortal dare?

Each ghostly form was now arrayed

In beauty, such as when God made

Man in his perfect loveliness;

Like to His image all express.—

The arid earth—now rich in bloom,

The zephyrs loaded with perfume;

The asphodel—more white than snow;

The amaranth, with purple glow;

The Syrian lily, which did fling

Contempt on Egypt's gorgeous king,*

(When in those regal robes attired,

Which reverential praise inspired;)

All mingling—did aroma lend

The balmy air—delight to send

Far as those tepid gales could blow;

And sweetest odours wafted throw

Round every hill, and distant vale:

That all their fragrance might inhale.—

The trees, with freshest foliage crowned,

Swept gracefully unto the ground;

While chorus-birds their shade amid,

(As if each other they out-did,)

Sang in such ecstasy—their throats

Could scarce trill forth the harmonious notes.—

* St. Luke xii. 27.

While rivulets—lit by the sun,

O'er pearly pebbles which did run,

Murmured in unison most sweet ;

This woodland concert to complete :

Soon drowned in the triumphant strains,

" The Lord Omnipotent now reigns !"

Which to those harps were joyful sung,

Once on those drooping willows hung,

When " Israel's sweetest singers," were

In Babylon bowed in mute despair,

Beside its brooks—remembering thee,

O Zion ! in prosperity !*

Attuned, by those late silent ghosts,

Melodious to the Lord of Hosts !

Was it the chaplets round their brow,

Which rendered them so radiant now ?—

Or hallelujahs which were breathed

By lips that smiles of rapture wreathed,

* Psalm xxxvii. 2.

Lending their face that charm divine

Of blended love, and faith benign ?—

It was not envy which depressed

My sad soul, sinking in my breast ;

It was despondency more grave,

Which holiest sympathy did crave.—

I, who from them had prompt recoiled,

Felt now by me they would be soiled ;

And, self-abhorent, stole away ;

(Poor leperous worm of spotted clay !)

I had not dared to lift mine eye,

To the supernal Majesty,

Who had redeemed them from despair :

I had but felt His presence there.

I had not dared to lift mine eye,

To the immense Eternity,

Whither such countless Just have flown ;

The precious ones, God calls His *own*.—

O Grand ! O vast Superlative !

What words can limit to thee give ?

What words convey how great thou art?

Illimitable!—not a part

Towards an end doth terminate!—

O thought! how mean, inadequate,

Art thou, when thou presumest to try

To girdle-in Infinity!

Thy ocean ebbs towards no shore—

In vain may telescope explore

To scan horizon, sweeping far

Into the depths of some dimmed star.

Thou independent planet-sphere,

Self-balanced—dost to nought adhere;

For all, inferior unto thee,

Would crumbled by thy contact be!—

Yet—*there* for me will be a place,

When I, too, am redeemed by Grace!

When disembodied from the grave

My spirit, which Christ died to save,

To immortality shall rise,

And penetrate ethereal skies!—

When I shall see, as once he saw,

Whose vision-mind was clear from flaw,

The Thrones—the Glories—Cherubim—

Rapt reverie revealed to him ;*

And all the marvels, prophet-saint,

Which thou couldst gaze on, and couldst paint.

Oh ! as the skies night's clouds invest,

Which canopy a world at rest ;

The curtains which young morn draws back,

With hand that leaves a fiery track,

To brighten till consummate day

Its full refulgence doth display !—

Now darkness quits the lustrous skies :

On which, at length, I bend mine eyes,

To hail the advent of that ray,

Which ushers in my ENDLESS Day !

* Rev. iv. 3.

I HAD A HOPE—'TIS GONE!

Oʜ! let us cease this child-game, "hide and seek,"

   This dodging round the corners of the heart;

If thou repentest of our plightings, speak:

   And we will, without added torture,—part!—

My mood is not to love, nor hate, in sport,

   Passions are serious in their due degree;

And I disdain the cowardly resort

   Of jest, to screen an earnest perfidy.—

Thee I approach as if for doom it were,

   With heart that hurries, then retards its

     speed;

And sombre whisper seems to bid, " prepare

   For word will instant break Hope's bending reed !"

I feel the derelict of some dire ban,

   Under the anger of thy distant eye ;

Which doth my conscious rectitude unman,

   Thee making guilty, yet unknowing why.

Oh ! so reliant is my soul, it blinks

   The question of a doubt, would kill me quite ;

And it, like charity, no evil thinks

   Of one, it *ever* would have in the right.

What I have borne !—yet, yet did I disclose

   The wrongs which make it agony to live ?

The wrongs which cause thee to be blamed by those

   Who suffer nothing from the pangs they give !

'Twas thou, in usurpation of Love's power,

   Obtained for me the pity, soothes me not !—

Oh ! when the autumn storm doth darkest lower,

   Leave then its battered flower to careless rot !—

How canst thou utterly forget to feel

    The sympathy, to trifles once lent weight ?

Yet Death doth laugh, when grates the vessel's keel

    Upon the rock, lets out its living freight.—

And treachery wears its very bitterest smile,

    The victim of its fraud when it beholds,

Writhing beneath the mockery of each will,

    As late conviction falsity unfolds !—

It is no trial for the callous heart

    To wrench the faith, another's joy secured ;

Yet—Heaven forbid ! thine e'er should feel the smart,

    The pain which teaches, that is then endured !—

Oh ! never may that torpid heart awake

    To the keen horror, quickens to remorse ;

To ponder on the ruin it doth make

    When it, for Mercy's, uses Tyrant's force.

Strange ! a pale girl, with eyes lid-veiled and meek,

    Such concentrated sternness can conceal ;

Nor one swift flushing o'er her marble cheek

    The hard resolve an instant but reveal !—

But he to solve such mystery who tries,

    In the endeavour "spends his strength in vain ;"

For the solution far too hidden lies

    For heart-ache's guessing, or for rack of brain !

This in a creature, fragile, delicate,

    As earliest primrose, bares its bloom to spring ;

Yet mighty in her strength to arbitrate

    Betwixt the causes Love and Fear do bring.

A thing, each manly hand would stretch to aid,

    So feeble, so defenceless, she appears ;

Yet, like a Sovereign, will be e'er obeyed :

    Whose throne despotic servile terror rears,

Who, with a glance can shine or shade impart,

    To warm, to chill, (as wilful whim doth move ;)

The mortified, forgiving, puppet-heart,

    Which is the bond-slave of despising Love !

THE MOTTO.

IT came, remembrance to awake
From opiate trance of apathy;
The seal of secrecy to break
On document of mystery;
And bade me read with glaring eyes,
The page which turpitude concealed;
Where gross, unrighteous perjuries,
By conscience to the soul revealed,
Made guilt convicted stand aghast,
As if there were stern witness by,
To prove the horrors of the past,
Present remorse doth amplify;

And sent a thrill throughout the frame,

    An agony from terror bred ;

Old " Motto!" at thy startling name,

    As whisper of the shrouded dead !—

A voice, to check my wild career;

    A warning as by Mercy given ;

As if a spirit hovered near,

    Too restless for the calm of Heaven ;

A mother's spirit !—could it rest,

    If conscious of my deeds below ?—

Would not that region of the blest

    A desperate anguish o'er it throw ?—

"All's well !"—Alas ! it had been so,

If I had died long,—long ago,—

For every added year to me

Hath been an added infamy ;

Like him the demons entered in,

To load with sevenfold weight of sin,

N

Until I dare not even survey

That from which Mercy turns away;

And whereto Pity doth deny

Her common tear of charity;

She, who hath wept Man's fall and crime,

Since Error owed its birth to Time!

Tush!—shall the "motto on a seal,"

Me so unman?—But, soft! I feel

A dear, despised, fond hand impressed

The words of fire, consume my breast!—

She flashed upon me like a beam

Of morning sun on heavenly dream;

As if to instant realize

That radiant vision of the skies;

The faithful love of those pure days,

It were profane in me to praise;

There's such a cloud betwixt their light,

And my soul's dim, obscuring night!—

She spake of peace,—of peace, for *me!*—

Of love, could that but mocking be?—

Her tone was serious,—and her eye

More mournful than when infants die;—

She said, "I might once more regain

My innocence, though crime did stain

My name, my nature with a blot;"

To *her* my *crime* had *she* forgot?—

I could have struck her, in the ire

These seeming tauntings did inspire;

Yet she persisted, till to Hope

I turned, as doth the heliotrope

To the bright sun;—and strength was

    there,—

To burst from folly's tangling snare.—

Is she of earth?—I've waited long,

To catch the angel-uttered song,—

Recalling the stray seraph here,

Home to her own celestial sphere;

And listened, with a throbbing heart,

For her blessed summons to depart;

And fainted with expectant dread;

Such beauty on my soul she shed.

But still I see her by my side,

A creature spreading far and wide

The influence of a holy life;

And most on me, my pardoning wife!—

She's made me not afraid to pray,

She's "showed me Heaven, and leads the way,"

She's reasoned down each doubt that rose,

She's taught me how to win repose,

She's told me Mercy would relent,

When sinners earnestly repent,

She's given me back my youth again,

My very youth, without a stain;

(And all this, giving back her love :

Oh! what contrition me doth move!)

She's forced me break that motto's spell,

To smile through tears, and cry, "ALL's

WELL!"

THE FRENCH AND ENGLISH ALLIANCE.*

DISSEVER not the new-formed tie,

Be it an ancient story;

The blood of Alma is not dry,

Of Inkermann's red glory;

Of Balaklava's gallant charge,

Where slaughter grew a fame;

And striplings' hearts did so enlarge,

They giants' hearts became;

Of Malakoff,—of the Redan,

When dauntless, side by side;

* "We cordially agree with our esteemed French contemporary, the 'Siécle,' of the 4th instant, that no better alliance can exist for England than that of France, and for France no more fruitful alliance than that of England."—MORNING POST, Nov. 6, 1856.

The French and English, to a man,

"On! on! to Victory!" cried.*

When French and English fearless fought,

When French and English bled;

As by one simultaneous thought

To conquest they were led.—

Their spirits still retained the fire,

Their wonted courage woke;

And, still intrepid in their ire,

Death's silent ranks they broke.

For those who saw their comrades fall,

Fought with increasing zeal;

As if the dead to them did call,

Their spirits to anele.—

* "Since Alma and Inkermann, sharing in a common danger
and partaking of a common glory, the French soldier has embraced
his British comrade as ' *bon drille, vieux camarade,*' and holds
him—and as a consequent, his nation—as the best and bravest
on earth, after the soldiers of *la belle France.*"—MORNING POST,
Nov. 6, 1856.

In trenches, which like rivers flowed,

Ran French and English blood;

From veins commingling tides bestowed,

Those sanguine streams to flood;

And in the Battle's hasty grave,

Repose in tranquil rest

The French and English,—which most brave

They neither sought to test.*

Can generous emotion seek

A dearer sympathy?

Even from their tombs those Heroes speak

To spirits bold reply!

---

* "At last the number in the trench is completed. The bodies lie as closely as they can be packed. Some of them have upraised arms, in the attitude of taking aim; their legs stick up through the mould as it is thrown upon them; others are bent and twisted into shapes like fantoccini. Inch after inch the earth rises above them, and they are left 'alone in their glory,'— no, not alone; for the hopes, and fears, and affections of hundreds of human hearts lie buried with them."—W. H. RUSSELL—BATTLE OF INKERMANN.

Their Union Death more rivetted.—

How sacred then appear

The wedded ashes, Honour sped

To the same envied bier !

And shall one dastard voice be raised,

Those ashes to malign ?—*

Where is the tongue that hath not praised

A friendship so divine ?—

Who enmity would dare invite,

Make foes whom friends we own ?—

Or pain the Living with a spite,

The Dead cannot atone ?

Oh ! shall a random word or two,

By reckless rancour hurled,

---

* " The French Government must be perfectly well aware that that of England has not the slightest power of dictating to, or controlling, the press ; and cannot therefore be made responsible for any course which it may be seen to pursue."—TIMES, Oct. 28, 1856. (*From the Manchester Guardian.*)

Divide the Warriors, who flew,

(When banners were unfurled,)

To fight—to triumph—and—to *die ;*—

Who heeded not, though they,

Unanimous for Victory,

In Death, *victorious* lay !

The French,—who equal danger shared,—

The French,—an equal fate,—

The French,—whate'er the English dared,

Did more than emulate !—

Cease that resentfulness of soul

Which burns to fiercest strife,—

As flames, enkindled past control,

Are with destruction rife !—

Spare, of the venerated dead,

The Testament of Truth ;

The blood in the Crimea shed

Bears witness of its sooth ;—

Think on the bravest of the Brave,

(Of such true Poets sing!)

Who fell those household gods to save,

To which pure bosoms cling!—

Oh! from barbarian Russia take

A lesson in your need;

And blush,—if contrast can awake

Remorse for venial creed;

Behold its homage for the dead;

Its honours to the brave;

The blood was not ignobly shed:

That winneth such a grave!*

Shall its rude serfs exult to hear,

How ye your dead revile?

---

* "The Russian dead at Sebastopol.   A letter from St. Peters-
burg, published in the 'Moniteur de l'Armée,' states that the sub-
scription opened in Russia for erecting a monument to the Russian
officers and soldiers killed at Sebastopol, has produced a sum of
60,000 silver roubles."—WEEKLY DISPATCH, Dec. 7, 1856.

Shall its rude serfs, with callous sneer,

    And cold, derisive smile,

Feel, how ye do avenge the shame

    Those Heroes on them heaped ;

When ye the Memory defame,

    In quenchless glory steeped ?

Remember, in your graceless scorn,

    Whate'er the Living be ;

The Dead are held, as the Unborn,

    Exempt from Calumny.—

And oh ! revere those did escape

    The carnage of that hour ;

The unstanched wounds, which then did gape,

    Appealed to Sovereign Power,

For the renown, ye would deny ;

    For the unfading prize

Of Glory, mounting to the sky,

    From Valour's sacrifice !

With hands which throb from ardent hearts

Entwine fresh laurels now ;

(The while the tear spontaneous starts ;)

To wreathe the Warrior's brow !

LOVE'S LIGHTEST STEP.

'NEATH moss-grown branches of old willow tree,
   In calm serene as Eden must have known;
Entranced I lay, in dream-wrought reverie,
   Which at vivacious life had instant flown.—
Picture on picture rose;—such visions rare,
   As fancy, love-inspired, can but portray;
Them to mere fancy I may well compare,
   Melting, alas! unrealised, away!—
Nature a vacuum ever doth abhor,
   Hence is it that the heart for ever aches;
For whate'er good it hath, a something more,
   Yet unpossessed, its full enjoyment makes.—-

How mine did yearn that pleasure to attain,

  Can but imagined be by one doth pine,

Like me, as earnestly that bliss to gain

  For which all other blessings he'd resign !—

How my soul stretched to reach the shadowy joy,

  Which still eluded its pursuing wing;

But to remember almost doth destroy,

  Though long it's ceased, a wearied, baffled thing!—

Softly as slumber stealeth o'er a child;

  Silent as wafture of a spirit's hand;

Noiseless as stream meanders through the wild

  Towards that sea, its tribute doth demand;

No rustling leaf pre-heralding her tread,

  She came behind me,—*She!* of whom I dreamed!—

(The aureole of Hope around my head,

  Resplendent as her eyes, must then have gleamed!)

Her velvet fingers pressing on mine eyes,

  (Whose voluntary touch made my heart bound,)

"Guess who I am!" with silvery laugh she cries;

  "Say! is the pearl for thy heart's casket found?"

"Ah! were mine eyes in utter darkness sealed,
  That heart would still discern all it absorbs;"
I murmured fondly, "for love e'er revealed
  The idolized unto the mental orbs;
And thrill, as it doth now, as tangled threads
  Of streaming, radiant hair, swept o'er my face;
The web of witchery, which Beauty spreads,
  Its captives, closely round, to interlace!"
My praises struck the key-note of her pride,
  And pitched the tone of its high privilege;
Now, conscious made of power, will she abide
  By her more ignorant, though sacred pledge?—
Dare I complain, if, for that hour intense,
  Years of intenser anguish did succeed?—
No,—it forestalled regret,—and each gross sense
  Etherialized,—as of earth's suffering freed!—
Yet she was but a mocking-bird, who sang
  Love's Sabbath-music, in that hour divine;
Yet with such truth, alas! the discord rang,
  That confidence supreme in it was mine!—

Hers was the syren-warbling doth betray

    The simple hearts which hear it to their harm;

O'er mine it held the strong, impulsive sway

    Of fascination's inexpressive charm.—

They who've ne'er loved so much may haply
    think,

    I might have been more wary—true! I might!—

The desert-parched, howe'er, the shipwrecked, drink

    Of the first water meets their straining sight;

Nor stop the stagnant stream to analyse,

    Until their maddening thirst they have allayed;

When the palled stomach at the draught doth
    rise,

    For which to Heaven in agony they prayed.—

So the love-fevered heart, in eager haste,

    Its Circe-cup, doth quaff as gratefully;

Sweeter than nectar seeming to the taste:

    But, oh! the bitter dregs at bottom lie!—

The sun doth never after shine so bright,

   When love hath trusted been and hath deceived!—

The heart doth never after feel so light,

   When of Hope's buoyancy it is bereaved !—

The earth a sadder, gloomier aspect wears,

   Enlivened not by memory of the past ;

And life unto the grave the shadow bears,

   Which, pall-like, over it in youth, was cast !—

So near the isthmus,—near the narrow strait,

   Which Heaven connects with this sublunar
      sphere;

Where Love, and all Love doth anticipate

   Is laid by Time upon Affection's bier ;

Need I lament the failure of my life ?—

   The loss of that which gave my being fire ?—

Which warmed the soul to overcome each strife ;

   From which the cold and listless prompt
      retire ?—

Can it now signify, that Fate refused

  To crown my hopes?—those boyish hopes, so fair !

Though "fine the gold" of love, it had been used,

  Beyond a hope its lustre to repair !—

It doth ! it doth ! for pleasure once possest,

  Though gone for ever, is a joy still felt ;

Glowing on the pure altar of the breast,

  As setting sun night's clouds with radiance belt !

THE GREAT GARNERER.

DREAD Husbandman! who never dost relax

Thy ever-grudging servants still to tax!—

Who add'st, each instant, to thy boundless store;

Yet—with gaunt greedy hands, up garnerest more!

Insatiate cravings rend thy famished breast,

And Plenty only lends imagined zest

Unto the Feast, which never satisfies,

But, like prodigious Wealth, new wants supplies.

Nor choice, nor dainty thou,—for thou canst feed

Upon the offal of each guilty deed;

Partaking, with the murderer, of blood,

And from the gibbet even accepting food;

Yet,—nice at times, the richest, ripest fruit,

Thy wishful, wilful palate will but suit;

Seasoned with tears,—with frantic prayers, for grace :

Lo ! from such banquet angels turn the face,

And Pity, clasping Sorrow to her heart,

Looks hopeless on, then slowly doth depart :

While revelry abhorrent shakes the skies,

To which Despair for retribution cries.

Thy Harvest gatherest thou, the whole year round,

And for the Grave are sheaves perpetual bound ;

All seasons are alike, alas ! to thee ;

Thou, licensed Purveyor, the tomb dost fee !—

Thou sendest forth thy mowers, mute and grim,

When Winter's mists Orion's lustre dim ;

When Spring's cold bosom chills the flower it wakes :

When Summer's breath parches the rill-fed lakes ;

And Autumn's vertical, down-glowing blaze,

The herbage burns, till not a kine can graze.—

Yet, yet they reap for thee, those mowers fell,

And labour on unwearied, nor one spell

Of rest luxurious take from endless toil;

While thou, as all unwearied, count'st the spoil.

The babe in fragrant slumber softly lies,

Which yet the mother's ever-gazing eyes

With wonder furnishes—as beauties new

Break on her startled and enraptured view.—

The babe so yearned for, hoped in, prized, caressed,

The babe for whom her dreams went oft in quest;

For whom each wakeful fancy eager sped:

Hush! hush! can she believe it? lieth dead!—

The Bridegroom-lover presses to his breast

The wife just made his own, and hath confessed,

In that low whisper of entranced bliss;

(The Heavens do hear, though Earth doth often
      miss;)

That there *is* happiness for man below:

That this is *not* a scene of endless woe.—

A moiety of Life she cost to win,

Yet he now deems his life doth but begin.—

Then comes a change o'er that bright, beaming face,

A little shadow, yet its cause how trace ?

A pallor o'er its blush ; a dull, strange look,

By Love, though blind, which cannot be mistook ;

His precious one is drooping,—she *will* die :—

The pang of that prophetic agony !—

Ah ! frenzied husband ! vainly bar the door !—

He'll enter in,—he *must* :—cease to implore !—

He but demands his rights—dominion,—power,—

O'er *all* of Earth, since the disastrous hour

Sin brought Decay unto each withering thing,

Which, doomed to die, to life will closer cling.

'Tis Nature's progress,—Fiat,—destiny ;—

Irrevocable—bare Humanity ;—

It is the summons that's despatched by Fate,

Alike for innocent and reprobate ;

The love-preserved,—the fortune-cast-away,—

The household angel,—and the shore-washed stray.

The new-born infant, with ambrosial breath,

And old decrepit, vassals are of Death.—

The Conqueror, to be conquered at the last,

The King, whose kingdom will be of the *Past*,—

O joy ! a limit's set to one, whose reign

The boldest awes, and dares him to disdain !—

Yet,—who'll survive, to signal his defeat ?

With shout triumphant, who his ear will greet ?

None ? Oh, what none ! Say you, the World will be

Again a chaos, less vitality ;

With every vestige of creation fled ;

" And darkness but the burier of the dead ?"

—Immortal Man, redeemed from mortal thrall,

Restored to Sonship with the SIRE of All,

Beholds the generations as they rise,

New Earths, new Heavens, new Eternities !

THE END.